It wasn't really the thought of the ball that was giving her breathing difficulties.

It was the thought of going with *him*. She blinked, struggling to shake the fanciful thought loose. She was his event planner. An event planner she wasn't even sure he really liked very much. She must have misunderstood him.

"Katherine," he said, the lip quirk turning into another slow smile. "Do you mind if I call you Katherine?" Conall asked, getting up to walk around his desk and perch on the corner of it—right in front of her.

"Katie," she murmured. He was so close she could see the dimple in his cheek peeking from the five-o'clock shadow.

"Sorry?" he said.

"Katie." She cleared her throat to stop her voice from rising even more. "People call me Katie. No one calls me Katherine."

"That's a shame. Katherine suits you better," he said.

"You can call me Katherine if you'd rather," she replied, her voice so breathless now she was surprised she hadn't passed out.

"Good. So, just to be crystal clear, it's you I'm asking on a date, Katherine. No one else."

Secrets of Billionaire Siblings

When you have everything money can buy,
love is hard to find...

Conall O'Riordan: he's a powerful, ruthless billionaire, jet-setting around the world managing his agricultural technology empire. But once he was penniless, raising his teenage sisters, Carmel and Imelda, alone! Now they're all grown up and still causing him grief. With their welfare still his number one concern, he's desperate to uncover their shocking family secrets...

For Conall, hiring event planner Katie Hamilton seems to be the best way to help his sister. But when the spark between him and Katie is out of control, he soon has another proposition to put to her...

Read Conall and Katie's story in
The Billionaire's Proposition in Paris

And look out for Carmel's and Imelda's stories

Coming soon!

Heidi Rice

THE BILLIONAIRE'S PROPOSITION IN PARIS

HARLEQUIN® PRESENTS®

Recycling programs for this product may not exist in your area.

ISBN-13: 978-1-335-56913-4

The Billionaire's Proposition in Paris

This edition published by arrangement with Harlequin Books S.A.

For questions and comments about the quality of this book, please contact us at CustomerService@Harlequin.com.

Harlequin Enterprises ULC
22 Adelaide St. West, 40th Floor
Toronto, Ontario M5H 4E3, Canada
www.Harlequin.com

Printed in U.S.A.

USA TODAY bestselling author **Heidi Rice** lives in London, England. She is married with two teenage sons—which gives her rather too much of an insight into the male psyche—and also works as a film journalist. She adores her job, which involves getting swept up in a world of high emotions; sensual excitement; funny, feisty women; sexy, tortured men; and glamorous locations where laundry doesn't exist. Once she turns off her computer, she often does chores—usually involving laundry!

Books by Heidi Rice

Harlequin Presents

Claimed for the Desert Prince's Heir
A Forbidden Night with the Housekeeper
Innocent's Desert Wedding Contract

Hot Summer Nights with a Billionaire

One Wild Night with Her Enemy

Conveniently Wed!

Contracted as His Cinderella Bride

Passion in Paradise

My Shocking Monte Carlo Confession

The Christmas Princess Swap

The Royal Pregnancy Test

Visit the Author Profile page
at Harlequin.com for more titles.

To my wonderful Irish father, Peter Ronan Rice, who died far too soon. He would have blushed like a nun if he'd ever had the chance to read this book! But he would have told me how much he enjoyed it anyway. Miss you always, Dad. xx

CHAPTER ONE

'I WILL NEED you to be on call twenty-four-seven. If I contact you, I expect you to make yourself available to me immediately...'

'Really?'

But I'm an event planner, not your mistress.

The whispered word—and the inappropriate thought—popped out before Katherine Hamilton could stop either, interrupting the stream of instructions she had been receiving ever since she had been ushered into Conall O'Riordan's glass-walled office on the thirtieth floor of Rio Corp's headquarters in London's golden mile five minutes ago.

She regretted the impulsive question immediately, when O'Riordan's dark head rose from the pile of papers on his desk—which he had been signing with efficient flicks of his silver pen as he reeled off his list of requirements—and his scorching blue gaze met hers for the first time.

Her breath backed up in her lungs—the jolt

of awareness both shocking and electrifying at the same time.

Oh... My!

She'd done her research as soon as she'd been told her fledging event-planning firm was in the running to receive a coveted contract from O'Riordan's company. She already knew Conall O'Riordan, the agricultural-tech billionaire, was strikingly handsome, renowned for his magnetism, drive, ambition and charisma. She knew he'd come from humble origins to become one of Ireland's most eligible men at the age of only thirty-one. But nothing could have prepared her for the impact of having that intense cobalt gaze focussed solely on her. Or the heat that slammed into her chest and spread through her body like wildfire.

Uncomfortable sensations she hadn't felt since Tom's death. Or, frankly, since before Tom's death. The wave of sadness which followed the thought of her dead husband helped her to catch her breath and examine her unprovoked reaction to O'Riordan.

Her relationship with Tom had not been a wild passion—not even close. It had been a childhood friendship that had blossomed into love. A love they'd never consummated. Physical intimacy had been the least of the things they'd lost when Tom had become ill. Did that explain her shocking reaction to O'Riordan—her chronic lack of sexual experience?

O'Riordan's brows rose as his lips flattened into a line but the intensity in his gaze didn't dim one iota… Could he feel it too—the shot of adrenaline turning her insides to mush?

I hope not.

'Did you say something, Ms Hamilton?' O'Riordan asked, or rather demanded, his husky tone, low with command, only increasing the devastating prickle of awareness.

Breathe, you ninny! And stop staring at his lips.

Katie struggled to collect herself and her shattered equilibrium.

This commission could be a game-changer for her company and life-changing for her. It was an opportunity she'd spent the last forty-eight hours prepping for with her team. She had a folder full of ideas propped next to her chair that they'd killed themselves to produce in record time, ever since receiving word of this interview from one of O'Riordan's management staff.

But, if she were to take this commission, they needed to establish some kind of working relationship—her shockingly inappropriate reaction notwithstanding.

She wasn't sure she liked the way O'Riordan had rattled off a string of outrageous demands. He hadn't even mentioned the event itself yet—

which she had been briefed was a team-building week followed by a company reception in O'Riordan Enterprises' Dublin headquarters.

This didn't feel like an interview, it felt like an interrogation.

'I… I wondered why you would need me to be available to you twenty-four-seven?' she managed.

'This is a problem?' he asked, his gaze raking over her with a raptor-like focus that only made her more aware of the wildfire still rushing over her skin.

Katie drew in a steadying breath.

He's just an extremely attractive and powerful man. It's instinctive. The female of the species is hard-wired to respond to the alpha male. It just means you're still human. Still alive. Still a woman. No biggie.

'No, not exactly, it's just…' she began, attempting to fill the awkward silence. 'Usually when I accept a commission I work up an event plan, then you and I and my team discuss it, and then—once you're entirely happy with everything—my team and I take over…' She paused, aware his focussed gaze was making her babble.

Was he trying to unnerve her? Because it was definitely working.

'It's my job to handle all the details,' she continued. 'So, basically, I wouldn't be doing my job properly if you felt you had to contact me in the middle of the night,' she finished, finally managing to get to something resembling a point.

He placed his pen on top of the papers he'd been signing. But then his lips quirked. It wasn't a smile, exactly, closer to a sneer. Unfortunately, it only made that striking combination of intensity and dark masculine beauty more breath-taking.

'I run an international company, Ms Hamilton. We're currently involved in projects in eight different time zones and I travel extensively. What is the middle of the night for you might be the middle of the day for me. I also never sleep more than three or four hours a night,' he added, then frowned, perhaps because he'd given away a piece of personal information. She shifted in her chair, the rush of sympathy at the admission he had insomnia as inappropriate as all the other sensations that had assailed her since she'd walked into his inner sanctum.

'If I have a question about the event,' he continued, having recovered from the slip a lot quicker than she had, 'I will want it answered. *Immediately.* By you. Not one of your staff,' he clarified, the tone both condescending and laser-sharp. 'If that kind of availability is a problem for you, we can end this interview now.'

'It's not a problem,' she said instantly. 'I can

be available if you need me to be. I'm just saying that shouldn't be necessary,' she added, aware she wanted this commission now more than ever, and not for entirely professional reasons.

Conall O'Riordan presented a challenge. Not just for her company but also for her. A challenge she had managed to avoid ever since Tom's death five years ago. Because in many ways she'd been dead too. She still wasn't ready to consider dating again. But navigating an inappropriate sexual attraction to a client—especially a client of Conall O'Riordan's calibre—was all part of the process of returning to the land of the living. Surely?

'Good, as long as we understand each other,' he said.

The tight feeling in Katie's chest released—a little. Her physical attraction to this man was nothing to be afraid of. Especially as there was no way on earth she'd ever act upon it. And no chance whatsoever that O'Riordan would ever see her in that way. From the copious research she'd done on him in the last forty-eight hours, she knew his dating history consisted mostly of supermodels and actresses and assorted other women who looked as sensational as he did.

She reached for the folder by her chair, desperate to direct their conversation back to where it needed to be. 'Would you like to see the concepts we were asked to put together for the event?' she asked, standing to place the folder on his desk. 'I understand it's for a week-long team-building event at your headquarters in—'

'It's not.'

'Excuse me?' She folded her arms over the portfolio and stood dumbly, staring at him, panic joining the unwelcome sensations still shimmering through her body.

Had Caroline Meyer, her assistant, got the details of the brief wrong? Surely not? Caro was brilliant, she didn't make mistakes. And, anyway, they'd spent forty-eight hours with very little sleep putting together this portfolio. If they'd got the brief wrong, there was no way he was going to give her this commission and all their work would have been wasted.

But, before she had a chance to spiral into a full-blown anxiety attack, he gestured for her to sit back down.

'I had you deliberately misinformed about the brief.'

'But…why?' she asked, not sure whether to be annoyed or astonished.

'Because I value my family's privacy, and I don't want information about the actual event or its location being leaked to the press. I'll expect you to sign an NDA before I hire you.'

'I… I understand,' she said, although she really didn't. Maintaining a client's privacy was part of any reputable event planner's DNA. Leaking that kind of information could destroy a company's reputation, especially a company like hers, which was hoping to plan exclusive, boutique events for a high-end clientele.

'Of course. I'll be more than happy to sign an NDA if that's what you require.' After all, it was just another of his unnecessary demands.

She knew how taciturn and demanding men like Conall O'Riordan could be, because her half-brother, Ross De Courtney, owned and ran the biggest logistic firm in Europe. Maybe Ross wasn't self-made like O'Riordan, having inherited De Courtney's from their late father. But Ross had the same drive and ambition, having grown the company's status and reach exponentially in the ten years he'd been its CEO, and he had the same demanding, inflexible personality.

But she'd never had to organise an event for Ross. She hadn't even been a part of his life for five years, ever since their epic falling out over her marriage.

'What you feel for Tom isn't love, it's pity, Katie. You're nineteen. I refuse to give you my permission to do something so ludicrous. And I'm certainly not paying for a wedding.'

'I don't need your money for a wedding, or

anything else, and I certainly don't need your permission.'

She swallowed the lump of anxiety that always surfaced when she thought of the angry words they'd exchanged, and how easy it had been for Ross to cut her out of his life. Just like their father…

Katie sliced off *that* unhelpful memory before it could take root, knowing it would only make her feel shakier.

So not the time, Katie.

Clearly spending two sleepless nights working on her now redundant portfolio had not been the best preparation for this meeting.

O'Riordan wasn't her estranged, dictatorial billionaire half-brother—or the father who had refused to acknowledge she even existed. He was a billionaire client. They had no personal connection.

Thank goodness. Working with O'Riordan would give her a unique insight into this kind of commission, all part of the steep learning curve she needed to be on to snare clients of his calibre.

'But I'm afraid I'd need to know what the event actually is,' she said. 'Before I can work up a proper proposal,' she finished, just in case he thought she was some kind of magician and could pull proposals out of her hat without doing the necessary groundwork with her team.

She sat down and placed the unopened and now entirely pointless portfolio beside her chair.

'No need to bid for it. You've got the commission,' he said.

Astonishment came first, swiftly followed by the buzz of achievement. Her heart bounced into her throat. 'Truly?' she said. And then wanted to kick herself.

Way to sound totally unprofessional, Katie.

His lips quirked again in that almost-smile, which did mad things to her bouncing heart rate. But as he spoke the nerves and the sizzle of sensation returned.

'Yes,' he clarified. 'I want this event to be tailored specifically to my needs, to make a statement befitting the O'Riordans' standing in our community and in Irish life. I spoke to Karim Khan about the baby shower you organised for his wife, Orla, last month,' he added, mentioning the biggest job Hamilton Events had done so far. 'Before the birth of their son. He recommended you.'

'I loved doing that event.' Katie smiled, remembering the last-minute commission she'd got through a friend of a friend in the Irish racing community. It had been Hamilton Events' first foray into the echelons of top society events and had given her the courage to start pitching for other similar work. 'They're a wonderful couple,' she added.

The nerves continued to jiggle and jump in her stomach, however.

The Khans' baby shower had been a small, intimate family affair—albeit for an extremely exclusive client. Karim Khan was a billionaire businessman, and also Arab royalty, having assumed the throne of Zafar several years ago now. His marriage to Orla Calhoun—the oldest daughter in the Calhoun racing clan—had been a match made in celebrity heaven two years ago.

From what O'Riordan had just said about his event, though, it didn't sound as if he wanted small or intimate.

'We can discuss the fee once everything has been finalised,' he continued, still not mentioning what the event was. 'But I'm prepared to pay double your usual rate as long as all my demands are met, which I understand to be ten percent of the budget.'

'That's correct. If you're not willing to talk about the actual event, it would be great to get an idea of the budget and how many guests you're expecting,' she said. At least if she had an idea of costs she could get a handle on the logistics.

'Whatever it takes,' he said, in that matter-of-fact tone which told her money really was no object. 'But I had a ballpark figure of five million euro. And a guest list of approximately a hundred and fifty people.'

'I see,' she said, trying to remember to breathe again.

A budget that size would give Hamilton Events a commission big enough to expand and get new offices in Central London. She loved the quirky converted railway buildings they currently inhabited in Shoreditch, in trendy East London, but it sent out the wrong vibe to the clients she was looking to attract. Much more than the money, though, this event could be a stepping stone to get Hamilton Events into the big league.

Standing up, he extended his hand. 'Deal?'

It wasn't really a question, but she nodded anyway and popped out of her seat.

His fingers curled around hers in a strikingly firm, unyielding grip, and the wildfire flared again. Her thigh muscles tightened and her palm burned before he let her go.

'Would you like to tell me what the event is, or wait until I've signed the NDA?' she asked, discreetly rubbing her burning palm on her thigh.

It's a job, Katie. A really, really good job. Stop freaking out.

His head tilted to one side but, just when she was convinced he might be able to tell how unsettled she was, he shrugged.

'It's a wedding.'

The word reverberated in her skull. She had always avoided doing weddings because they reminded her of the first and only wedding she'd ever planned. Her own. To Tom. Ten days before he'd died of the rare cancer which had snuck into his body a year before their wedding day—and had slowly robbed them of the lives they might have had.

'You're getting married?' she asked to stop herself from blurting out the truth.

Did he know she'd never planned a wedding professionally? Would he withdraw the offer if she told him? How was she going to cope with arranging all those details, that she'd once done for love, for a man like him? Who appeared to be as coldly unemotional as he was compelling?

The thought felt strangely intimate, when it absolutely wasn't… Which was only making her freak out more.

He laughed, the deep chuckle as bitter as it was amused.

'Absolutely not,' he said. 'It's a wedding for one of my sisters. I have two of them,' he said, the muscle in his jaw relaxing for the first time.

Her heart slowed, despite her best intentions. However cold and cynical this man appeared to be, he wasn't as cold and cynical as her brother, because he clearly cared deeply about his sisters.

She steeled herself against the wayward emotions at the warmth in his eyes. Just because Conall O'Riordan loved his sisters, enough to pay for an extremely lavish wedding, didn't make him—or planning this event—any less of a threat to her peace of mind. Or any less of a logistical nightmare. Even she knew securing a suitably stunning venue for a society wedding for a hundred and fifty guests two months before the event would be next to impossible.

'Her name's Imelda,' he said, interrupting Katie's thoughts. 'She's twenty-one and has made the insane decision to marry her childhood sweetheart. Who happens to be a local farmer near my home in Connemara. I don't approve,' he added somewhat unnecessarily given the disapproval dripping from every word. 'But she's headstrong, as well as a hopeless romantic, so I'm stuck with the situation and I've decided to let her use Kildaragh,' he finished.

Katie's mind whirred to a stop. She'd seen photos of Kildaragh Castle while researching O'Riordan in the last few days. The mostly Victorian building built on the ruins of a medieval monastery on Ireland's untamed west coast was stunning.

At least she wouldn't have to find a venue, then. Sourcing all the necessary services might still be quite challenging, but she would just have to call in every favour she'd ever had.

Then something he had said reverberated in her head. 'Is it your sister's marriage you don't approve of, or the relationship?' she blurted out.

He frowned, and she knew she'd overstepped the mark. But to her surprise he answered her.

'Both, Ms Hamilton. Imelda is young enough to believe the usual nonsense about love. Which is why she's too young to make this decision. But, even if she weren't, she'd still be making a mistake. I have nothing against farmers, and Donal's a nice enough lad but he lacks ambition. He's not good enough for her.'

'So you don't believe she's in love?'

'No, I don't—not least because romantic love doesn't really exist. It is simply a construct used to trap the unwary,' he supplied. 'And separate people from their hard-earned cash.'

It was a view so cynical she almost felt sorry for him. How could anyone go through life genuinely believing something so hopeless? She'd had the love of her life and lost him. And it had nearly destroyed her. She didn't expect to find another. Nor did she really want to. It would feel like cheating on Tom. But it saddened her to think that men like O'Riordan and her brother just didn't get that…for all their wealth and success.

'And to glorify the most basic of urges,' he added.

His mouth crinkled again in that coldly compelling almost-smile. And suddenly the atmosphere became charged. Charged with the shocking sensations that had derailed her as soon as she had arrived. His gaze roamed over her, penetrating, provocative and disturbingly intimate. Her body quickened in response, mortifying her.

'But you're still willing to pay a fortune to celebrate a marriage you don't approve of?' she blurted out, desperate to break the tension.

'Whether I approve or not, it won't stop Imelda making this mistake,' he said. 'And, anyway, why would you question that impulse, seeing as you're going to make a killing out of it?'

'Because I do believe in it,' she said, trying not to be offended by the remark.

'Believe in what, exactly?' he asked. 'Spending a fortune on a wedding?'

'No, in marriage,' she said. 'And love.'

He blinked, and she could see the flash of surprise in his eyes before he masked it.

'How quaint,' he said. 'And convenient—coming from a wedding planner.'

She wasn't a wedding planner—not yet, anyway. And she wasn't in the business of convincing her clients to believe in love. She might have been as hopelessly romantic as his sister once but she was a realist now. She'd had to become one.

But, even so, she couldn't quite let the caustic comment pass.

'Perhaps, but at least it means you'll get your money's worth,' she said. 'Because I'll do my absolute utmost to make sure Imelda's special day is one she'll remember for the rest of her life.'

'Or until she gets divorced,' he supplied, but then added, 'But it's grand you intend to ensure I get my money's worth, because I always insist on getting what I'm paying for.'

His gaze remained focussed on her, and she had the strangest feeling they weren't talking about his sister's wedding any more. The atmosphere was crackling now with an electrical energy that was forcing her dormant body to wake up… In a way it had never been woken up before.

He sat and picked up his pen, his gaze returning to the papers on his desk.

'My assistant will be in touch with more details once you've signed the NDA,' he murmured as he began scanning the documents again and signing them.

Her body sunk, like a puppet released from its strings, the loss of his attention almost as jarring as having been the centre of it moments before.

'I'm taking the company chopper to Kildaragh next Friday—you can accompany me for the week to check out the venue and organise the details. I'd like to have everything finalised by the end of that week.'

'You want a wedding for a hundred and fifty people organised by the end of next week?' she asked, so shocked she wasn't sure how to respond. Did he realise he was asking the impossible? Planning any event took time and consideration. Even with a venue secured there were so many details to consider and so many choices to make.

His gaze connected with hers, pulling the puppet strings taut again. And she had the strangest feeling he knew he was asking the impossible and that he was enjoying it. 'I do,' he said. 'It's a short time frame, but I expect you to make it work… If not I can withdraw the…'

'I can make it work,' she said. She would just have to hit the ground running when she got to Connemara.

'Good, work up some concepts in the meantime so I can look at them en route to Kildaragh.'

'Absolutely. Would it be okay if I brought some of my team with me…?' she ventured. At least if she had Caro there to chase down the details, and Trev, one of their regular freelance coordinators, to help check out local suppliers…

'No, you may not. I'd prefer you come alone. I don't want hordes of people in my home,' he said.

Caro and Trev would hardly be a horde, and

really, his home had to have about a hundred bedrooms, from the photos she'd seen online, but again, she suspected this was a test. And she refused to fail it, so she immediately acquiesced again. She did not want to lose this commission on a technicality.

'I can work solo if you need me to.' And there was always email and online conference calling to keep her team in the loop.

He gave a barely perceptible nod, as if he had expected no less. 'By the way, no Christmas themes, even if the event is scheduled for the first week of December.'

She nodded. 'We can do something with a winter theme, rather than Christmas, if that's what you and Imelda prefer.'

'I do,' he said, and she noted the emphasis on the 'I'.

So, he had a problem with Christmas as well as romance. *Quelle surprise*. And he seemed to think he could do this without the bride's input. The softening she'd felt towards him earlier seemed increasingly misplaced.

His gaze dropped back to his papers. 'See yourself out,' he said, and she realised she'd been dismissed.

She left the office, ignoring the spurt of indignation at the cursory command, stupidly grateful to be away from that all-seeing gaze.

As she arrived in the lift lobby the view of St Paul's Cathedral dome thirty storeys below, the grey expanse of the River Thames and the Shard standing on the opposite bank like an enormous phallic symbol was almost as vertigo-inducing as the thought of her trip to Connemara in five days' time. And all the challenges presented by this commission… And more specifically her taciturn and tactless—and far too unsettling—new billionaire client.

Pressing the lift call button, she noticed her finger trembling. She curled her hand into a fist to stop the shaking. She needed to get her reaction to Conall O'Riordan under control ASAP, or how the heck was she going to survive being in close proximity to him for a week and behave with any degree of professionalism whatsoever?

Her heartbeat jammed into her throat. She swallowed convulsively.

Don't be ridiculous, Katie. You're a professional. O'Riordan's a client. Your best client ever, in fact. You've worked hard for this opportunity and you are not going to muck it up thanks to a few inappropriate sizzles.

And anyway, what were the chances Conall O'Riordan would be that hands-on? Surely he wouldn't actually want to be that involved in the wedding planning? He'd already made it clear weddings were not his area of interest or expertise. And he was an extremely busy man.

Imelda, being the bride, was the one Katie would ultimately be working for, no matter who was paying the bills.

Or how overbearing and controlling and ludicrously hot he happened to be!

CHAPTER TWO

'YOU'RE LATE!' CONALL shouted above the noise of the helicopter powering up as Katherine Hamilton appeared at the entrance to the rooftop heliport on top of O'Riordan Tower and rushed towards him. She carried a small bag and a much bigger folder, like the one she'd had with her five days before—probably full of ideas he intended to reject. But, as satisfaction settled over him at the thought of how much he intended to enjoy putting Ross De Courtney's sister in her place, her coat flattened against her body in the wind created by the helicopter's blades and an unwanted shot of desire fired through his body on cue.

He frowned, finally forced to acknowledge his decision to hire her—five days ago, for a wedding he still wasn't sure he wanted to follow through on, when the original plan had simply been to quiz her for information about her brother—had been impulsive in the extreme. And he was not an impulsive man.

As she approached, it occurred to him she was considerably shorter than the women he usually found attractive, her figure soft and curvy in places where theirs were toned and taut, which only made the buzz of reaction in his groin more annoying.

Dusk had fallen a few minutes ago, and the reddish glow from the sunset over the City of London gave an added lustre to her chestnut hair. As if it needed it. The unruly curls cut in a practical bob bounced, drawing his gaze to the light flush of exertion on her cheeks.

I wonder if she'd have the same glow on her skin after making love?

He tensed, irritated even more by the unbidden thought—and the realisation that his knee-jerk decision to invite her to Connemara had as much to do with her unruly effect on his libido as it did with her connection to a man he needed to find out a lot more about—as discreetly as possible.

Inviting the man's only known blood relation to an interview had seemed like the perfect solution. Until he'd lifted his head, seen the shock of awareness in her eyes and his libido had gone off like a firecracker, too.

He steeled himself as the unwanted buzz of attraction turned into a definite hum. What was it about Ross De Courtney's half-sister that made her so damn tempting, when he knew he shouldn't be tempted? And he certainly didn't want to be.

And what was it about her obvious awareness of him five days ago that had made her seem vulnerable when he knew she was not?

She was an astute and ambitious businesswoman—her boutique company already making an impression in the circles he frequented—but much more than that she was a De Courtney. Which meant, unlike his own sisters, she had been privileged, pampered and entitled her whole life, even if she kept her connection to De Courtney on the down low, and no matter how hard she might be willing to work.

Although that remained to be seen. Perhaps his fact-finding mission had faltered at the first hurdle during their initial interview… But by bringing her to Kildaragh, he had bought himself more time. So what if his motivations hadn't been entirely practical? The plan was still a good one.

He would put her through her paces on this assignment and discover how much of her success had been bought for her by her brother. Meanwhile, he would find out everything he could about the man who had exploited his sister—a man he was already convinced was better off out of his nephew's life. But he needed to be sure.

If Katherine Hamilton did a good enough job, he might even consider following through on the wedding plans—after all, he hadn't lied to her about being unable to stop Imelda making this mistake. But he very much doubted she'd be able to impress him that much.

Katherine's green eyes connected with his when she reached him and she sent him an eager and hopeful smile—apparently undaunted by his irritation.

'I'm so sorry, there was a problem on the Tube. It won't happen again, Mr O'Riordan.'

He stared at her flushed face. What the heck was she doing riding the Tube? Was this a bid to persuade him she was a regular Londoner, when they both knew she wasn't? That she'd had to struggle to get what she needed, as he had?

Yeah, right.

'No. It won't happen again,' he said, signalling to his assistant to take her carry-on bag and the unwieldy folder.

He cupped her elbow to lead her towards the chopper. And felt the satisfying ripple of reaction at his touch, the way he had five days ago, when they'd shaken hands. This time, though, he didn't drop his hand until he had directed her into the aircraft.

Perhaps it was counter-productive to get satisfaction from her reaction. After all, he wasn't a man like her brother, eager to prey on young women, but then he didn't feel she deserved any pity. She knew how the game was played. He'd sensed her arousal too, during their last merry meeting. Why not use this inconvenient attraction to his advantage to get poetic justice for what her brother had done to Carmel? And little Cormac.

'I'm a busy man, Ms Hamilton,' he said as he fastened his seatbelt. 'I don't like to be kept waiting.'

'Absolutely, I understand,' she said as she took off her coat to reveal a fitted pencil skirt and an emerald silk blouse which matched her eyes. The ensemble should have looked slick and professional, but somehow didn't. He noticed the way the silk clung to her full breasts and how a tendril of hair stuck to her lips. She brushed the errant curl back behind her ear and seated herself opposite him.

'If you're going to be late, contact my assistant Liam and let him know,' he said, annoyed by the fact the hum in his groin had only got worse. 'Or, better yet, be on time. I don't like doing business with people who can't be punctual.' He was being unnecessarily surly; after all she was less than five minutes late. But the truth was, he did hate to be kept waiting, especially by a woman like her. And he wanted to test her response.

How would she react to being put firmly in her place? *Again.*

Although, truth be told, her reaction during their interview to his overbearing behaviour hadn't been as productive as he'd hoped. In fact, he'd ended up revealing far more than he had intended about his attitude to love and marriage, and even about his relationship with Imelda, of all things.

But he'd decided after she'd left, that all the starry-eyed romantic nonsense she'd spouted and those probing personal questions had just been part of her act. Of course a high-end wedding planner would pretend to be a romantic. She certainly couldn't know about his sister's connection to Katherine's brother. Not even Carmel was aware he had found out the truth a week ago about the identity of Cormac's father… *Yet.*

Even so, he shouldn't have let Katherine Hamilton's little act get a reaction out of him. And certainly not enough to engage in a personal discussion.

It wouldn't happen again.

She blinked, her gaze as guileless and earnest as it had been in his office. Damn, but she was good at her act. No wonder he'd momentarily fallen for it.

But then her gaze flashed with impatience.

Finally, he'd got to her.

Not so placid now, are we, Ms Hamilton? Let's see how long it takes you to show your true colours. And lose this commission.

But to his surprise she didn't rise to the bait. Instead the flicker of resistance disappeared and she said simply, 'As I said, I understand. I won't be late again. This commission means a great deal to me and my company. I want to get everything right. And I promise you, I will.'

He heard the sincerity again in her voice. And the eagerness and enthusiasm, which made him feel like a bastard—even though he knew she deserved his disdain… She was just another daughter of the elite playing at being a businesswoman. Seriously, could she have come up with anything more unoriginal than working as a party planner?

But how had he been so easily outplayed—and made to feel in the wrong, when he wasn't?

'I intend to hold you to that promise,' he said, but the threat lacked any heat. Somehow she'd defused the situation, which only annoyed him more.

She leant down to clasp the folder Liam had left by her seat after he'd taken her coat. 'Would you like to have a look at the themes my team and I have been putting together?' she asked, launching into a professional spiel, belied somewhat by the chemistry thickening the air between them. She opened the folder and he got glimpses of colours and fabrics, sketches and notes, and some photos of Kildaragh she must have downloaded from the internet. 'Obviously, until I've had a chance to properly assess the venue,' she said. 'And spoken to Imel—'

'We'll have time for that tomorrow.' He cut her off, still annoyed. He certainly didn't intend to let her speak to Imelda, not until he had made a final decision whether to use her services or not. He reached into his jacket pocket to pull out his phone. 'I need to make some calls. We'll be at Kildaragh in about three hours. Until then I'd prefer it if you didn't disturb me.'

Her cheeks heated and her eyes flared, finally supplying the temper he'd been hoping for earlier. But this time it didn't amuse him the way it might have done before, because it made those emerald eyes spark with a green fire that only made her colouring more striking. And the hum in his abdomen start to throb. *Damn.*

'Of course, Mr O'Riordan,' she said, and closed the folder with more of a snap than was strictly necessary.

Breaking eye contact, she turned to stare out of the window just as the helicopter rose into the evening sky. The bird banked as it climbed, giving them a panoramic view of the city at dusk. The Houses of Parliament and the Millennium Wheel, floodlit on the opposite bank, appeared like sentries to the city's achievements past and present as the aircraft followed the bend in the Thames to head west for the journey to Ireland.

He heard her breath catch, the way it had done once before in his office when he'd first made eye contact with her. The sound of staggered surprise had a similarly visceral effect on him now. And the throb of unwanted sensation arrowed down.

Her fingers gripped her arm rest and he shook his head to remove the sudden vision of those same perfectly manicured nails digging into his shoulders as she rode his...

Sweet Jesus. He thrust his fingers through his hair but was unable to take his eyes off her.

She crossed her legs, revealing a glimpse of thigh above the hem of her skirt. The heat flooding his groin became painful as he imagined placing his lips on the inside of her knee, nibbling his way up and finding out if he could make her gasp again, this time with pleasure.

He looked away, furious now.

Did she know what she was doing to him? Was this all part of the act?

He flipped open his laptop and began the series of calls he had scheduled for the flight, determined to ignore her for the rest of the journey.

Katherine Hamilton's attractiveness, and his reaction to it, was a complication. No question.

A complication he would have to address sooner rather than later, he decided when he caught a whiff of her scent. With notes of orange, cinnamon and rosemary, the addictive aroma was subtle and earthy, and not at all the sweet, cloying, expensive scent he would have expected.

But then everything about Katherine Hamilton had been unexpected so far. And he was fairly sure he didn't like it—one little bit.

Katie's eyelids fluttered open at the judder of turbulence and her gaze connected with Conall O'Riordan's. She pushed her hair back behind her ear and straightened in her seat, embarrassed to realise she'd nodded off after the light supper she'd been served. And he'd noticed. How long had he been watching her? And why did that just make the uncomfortable sizzles even worse?

'I'm sorry,' she murmured instinctively, because he was studying her again with that assessing gaze that made her feel as if she had something to apologise for, although she had no idea what.

She was still mortified she'd managed to be

late for their rendezvous at his heliport. And that he'd been so annoyed with her. She was never usually late for anything, certainly nothing as important as this assignment, but there was something about Conall O'Riordan that unnerved her quite apart from those sizzles… It was almost as if he were deliberately trying to provoke her with those unsettling looks and the curt commands.

She took in a careful breath. Let it out again.

For goodness' sake, Katie, get a grip. This isn't about O'Riordan—this is about you. You're just tired. And a little overwrought because you have a lot riding on this job.

Everything about this commission felt far too personal already—perhaps because of her daft and extreme reaction to O'Riordan, and the pressure to get this right. But that had nothing to do with him. She was projecting. And she needed to stop it.

After five fourteen-hour days working on themes and concepts for the wedding and sounding out suppliers, she wasn't her usual pragmatic, professional self, that was all.

He gave a slight nod, accepting her apology as if it were his due. Resentment flickered at his overbearing attitude. Yes, she'd been late, something she would make sure she never did again, and she was still struggling to make sense of her reactions to him, but he'd definitely overreacted.

As hard as it had been to hold her tongue, and not let his surly attitude get to her, she'd managed it. So she could take some solace from that. Clearly handling bad-boy billionaires was going to be much more challenging than she had assumed. But she could do this. She had to do this.

'We'll be arriving in ten minutes,' he said, the first words he'd spoken to her since dismissing her after take-off—and then ignoring her for the last two and a half hours. The husky Irish accent rippled down her spine, as it did every time he deigned to speak to her, even when he was chastising her, which seemed to be rather often.

She inclined her head and forced herself to smile. 'I'm looking forward to seeing your home,' she said, in another attempt to strike up something resembling a rapport with him.

She was usually so good at forming strong working relationships with clients. She'd always been a people person—which was why event planning had been such an obvious choice of profession. Surely, if she really put her mind to it, she could soften him up enough not to constantly be getting on his bad side?

'The pictures on the internet made the castle look quite magnificent,' she continued. 'Certainly a wonderful venue for a wedding. Your sister is very lucky.' Buttering him up was a strategy she hadn't used yet. But surely it had to be a good way to start knocking down the brick wall of his disapproval? 'I understand you bought it several years ago and spent a fortune renovating it, using local craftspeople to bring it back to its former glory.'

Sycophancy didn't seem to be working either, though. His deep-blue gaze remained unmoved and was as unsettling as it had been earlier—when he'd been telling her off for her tardiness, as if she were an unruly child instead of a capable businesswoman.

But then his lips quirked in that devastating almost-smile, which didn't warm his gaze so much as make it even more intense. Liquid sensation sank into her lap, and she crossed her legs, desperate to stem the flow.

'I see you've done your homework,' he remarked.

'I wanted to find out as much as I could about the venue before I arrived,' she admitted, because his comment hadn't exactly screamed approval for all her hard work. 'I read the interview you gave to *Investor's Weekly* two years ago after beginning work on the renovations. It sounded like a daunting and yet exciting project,' she added, determined to draw him out if it killed her.

'Expensive and time-consuming would be closer to the mark,' he said, directing his gaze back to his laptop and dismissing her again.

Whoever said the Irish had the gift of the gab had obviously never tried to talk to Conall O'Riordan in a snit. Her heartbeat continued to rise, though, as she took the opportunity to watch him unobserved—and tried to decipher what exactly it was about his appearance that unsettled her so.

Perhaps it was that rakish curl in the thick dark hair that fell across his brow and touched the collar of his shirt. Maybe it was the sculpted lips, the designer stubble—which looked entirely natural, rather than deliberate—and gave him a wild, untamed air.

Perhaps it was the harsh planes and angles of his face, both unyielding and commanding and perfectly symmetrical but for a small scar on his top lip. Or maybe it was the length of his eyelashes? she wondered, noticing them for the first time as he concentrated on typing something out on his phone with lightning-fast thumbs. Seriously, most women would kill for those eyelashes, so how was it that they only added to the striking masculinity of his face?

Stop ogling him, Katie. It's not helping.

She dragged her gaze away from O'Riordan and stared out of the window, while trying to drag her mind back on topic and ignore the pounding heartbeat which had settled disconcertingly between her thighs.

Seriously, what are you? A glutton for punishment? The man's an absolute pill, despite his staggering looks. Since when have you found arrogance attractive?

'If you look out the other window, you can see Kildaragh coming up now.'

Her head jerked round, startled by the quietly spoken instruction—and the unmistakeable note of pride in his voice. It was an olive branch, of sorts, but she grasped it with both hands, scooting round in her seat to peer out as the helicopter banked to their left. She didn't have to fake her enthusiasm, though, when Conall O'Riordan's home came into view.

'Oh… Wow!' she gasped.

The staggering beauty of Kildaragh Castle was not unlike its owner, so perfectly proportioned it was hard to believe it was real… The palatial vision was like something from a children's story book or a Hollywood movie. Towers and turrets pierced the night sky, joined by the elegance of fortified ramparts in an amalgam of different styles and periods which, she already knew from her research, were a legacy of the castle's illustrious past.

It had first been the seat of an Irish king, then

a monastery and then a boarding school, before falling into disrepair in the nineteen-eighties. The immaculate and extensive work Conall O'Riordan had had done to the building to bring it back to life was clear in every detail, highlighted by the silvery glow of the full October moon and the light from the arched windows as the helicopter approached.

'The pictures I found didn't do it justice,' she whispered, more to herself than him now, utterly captivated by the structure's artistry. 'It's absolutely gorgeous.'

She sighed. She sucked in another breath as she noticed a huge stained-glass window on what looked like a small chapel on the west side of the structure as the helicopter circled. Walled gardens covered the back of the estate and she could just about make out the cliff edge, where the promontory on which the castle was built dropped into the sea. 'Is that window original?' she asked, her artist's eye already in heaven as she swung back round to face him.

For the first time, she caught him with an actual smile on his lips—one that took the cynical chill out of his eyes and added a mesmerising dimple to his cheek.

A dimple? Seriously?

'No, the house and grounds were wrecked when I bought the place. There was stained glass there in the original structure, according to the records. The window was made by a young craftswoman on Innismaan called Elaine Doherty. She used original materials and did some research into the castle's history to come up with the images, which were inspired by the folklore surrounding the last High King of Ireland who, legend has it, built the first structure on this site.'

Pride thickened his voice and took away the cynical edge she had become accustomed to, which only made him more handsome.

'It's exquisite,' she said, trying to convince herself she was totally talking about the stained-glass window. 'She's very talented.'

She swivelled round in her seat to concentrate on the amazing architectural achievements of his home, rather than that mesmerising dimple, as the aircraft settled on the heliport constructed near the cliff edge.

As the blades powered down, the crash of surf on rocks became audible, full of drama and energy, not unlike the clatter of her heartbeat—excited not just at the prospect of the magnificent wedding she could plan here but also at the small sign of his approval.

Calm down, Katie. This is a job, not an adventure! However dramatic the setting and captivating the client.

'I can't wait to see it in daylight,' she added. 'And start planning how best to use the location. Does your sister have a preference for where the marriage service should be conducted?' she asked, subtly trying to introduce the subject of the bride, and already imagining how incredible it would be if Imelda wanted to get married in the chapel.

'I expect so,' he said. 'We can discuss all that tomorrow,' he added as the door opened from the cockpit and the assistant who had served her dinner appeared.

'Conall,' the young man said, surprising Katie by addressing his boss by his given name. 'Geraldine Ahern at Amari Corp wanted to know if you could take a conference call tonight with Karim about the Zafar project.'

'Sure.' He unclipped his seat belt and lifted his jacket off the seat beside him. After slipping on his coat, he indicated Katie. 'See Ms Hamilton into the house and introduce her to Mrs Doolan.'

At last he turned back to her, but the smile was gone and he was all business again, making her feel oddly deflated. 'I'll see you tomorrow at five to discuss the details further. If you need anything, speak to my housekeeper.'

The door to the helicopter was opened by the ground crew and the wild scent of sea and earth rushed in with a splatter of rain, the rumble of surf turning into a roar. Before she had a chance to thank him, or even get her breath back, he had disappeared down the aircraft steps and was already making his way into the house, surrounded by a coterie of people who had obviously been waiting for their arrival.

'I'll get your coat, Ms Hamilton,' the young assistant said.

'Thank you,' she murmured, unable to take her eyes off the retreating figure of her new client. Silhouetted against the castle's floodlit splendour, he looked almost mythical. His tall frame took the steps up to the heavy oak entrance door two at a time before he disappeared inside.

Like the lord of all he surveys. Literally.

She shook the thought loose and struggled to even her breathing. Then tried to figure out why she felt so giddy… And disorientated.

Maybe this was a job and not an adventure, but weirdly it felt like the latter. Surreal and challenging, but also unbelievably exciting…

And she had a bad feeling that had nothing to do with the commission—and the virtually impossible task of organising a major society wedding in two months for a couple she had yet to meet—and everything to do with the taciturn man who had just walked away from her. And was even more fascinating and overwhelming than his home.

CHAPTER THREE

KATIE WOKE EARLY the next morning in the palatial suite of rooms in the castle's west tower that had been assigned to her, feeling more than a little groggy after a not entirely peaceful night's sleep. Who knew her inappropriate reaction to her new client would chase her in dreams? Her sleep had been disturbed by sensual images of Conall O'Riordan looking tall and indomitable while commanding her to do a lot more than just organise a wedding for him.

Taking a fortifying gulp of sea air from her window—and enjoying the magnificent view of the deserted cove below the castle—she huffed out a determined breath.

Work—that was what she needed. To take her mind off Conall O'Riordan's impressive presence. And it wasn't as if she didn't have a ton of things to be getting on with. Before her scheduled meeting with Conall that afternoon, she wanted to be up to speed on as many details as possible. For starters she needed to assess the castle's facilities and the grounds, work up some informed suggestions about where to schedule the different elements of the event, liaise with her team to discuss the logistics—now she finally had a confirmed date via email from one of O'Riordan's army of personal assistants—and hopefully meet the bride.

Even though Conall still hadn't mentioned a meeting with Imelda, Katie felt that was the obvious next step. Imelda was the bride and surely she would want input on what kind of wedding this was going to be?

After jumping into the suite's power shower to wash off the last of her sleep haze, she dressed in jeans, boots and a smart sweater—all the better to check out the castle's extensive walled gardens and parkland while still appearing professional, just in case she bumped into her host.

It didn't take her long to track down the housekeeper, Mrs Doolan, who she had been introduced to the night before. Unlike her boss, Mrs Doolan, who insisted on being called Maureen, was a bubbly, chatty and welcoming soul who—after insisting Katie have a full Irish breakfast—was more than happy to give her a guided tour of Kildaragh.

Maureen introduced her to the ground staff and the castle's chef, Clodagh Murphy, who, strangely, had not yet been informed of the upcoming nuptials. Katie made a note to ask Conall if he wanted to hire an outside caterer or use Clodagh and her team with some supplementary kitchen and waiting staff.

While touring the castle, Katie was told that the east wing held Conall's offices, but according to Maureen and the other staff he was rarely in residence and neither of his sisters lived on the grounds either.

She took copious pictures and notes of the castle's two dining salons, four stunning antechambers and all the different reception areas in the two main wings, jotting down ideas and suggestions that she intended to incorporate into the themes and activities she had already worked out.

She also checked out the chapel, which could be an option for conducting the wedding itself. Not only was it beautifully appointed, right next to the castle—so even if it snowed there would be no problem getting people from the church to the reception afterwards—but it was tranquil and elegant. The stained-glass window she had admired the night before was illustrated with a king and his fairy court, only one of the building's many stunning features.

When Maureen showed her the castle's banqueting hall, Katie knew she had an equally perfect venue for whatever festivities Conall and his sister preferred for after the vows had been said—whether it be a formal sit-down meal or a more relaxed affair.

Four storeys high, the hall was as perfectly restored as the rest of the castle, from its vaulted timber ceilings, to the intricate stone carvings on the imposing walls, to the marble flooring and the bespoke mahogany furniture. She glanced around the magnificent chamber, imagining how amazing it would look once her floral and lighting designers had got to work, decorating the austere room with fresh winter blooms, candles and torchlight, and enough wow factor to bring out the venue's fairy tale appeal.

Conall O'Riordan might not be a romantic, but she knew his sister was, and his home would provide the perfect place to give her marriage a start fit for a fairy queen.

'Would you like me to serve you lunch, Miss Hamilton? It's past two o'clock and you must be starving.'

Katie glanced up from her smart phone, where she had been jotting down notes to share with her team, to find Maureen standing at the entrance to the hall.

'Oh… Goodness,' she said, saving herself from swearing just in time. 'Is it already two o'clock?' She had less than three hours before she was due to meet with Conall and she had yet to make contact with his sister. 'I would love a sandwich or something, if it's not too much trouble. But what I really need to do is maybe talk to Imelda. The bride. I'd love to arrange to meet her—and hopefully her fiancé—at some point.'

Conall really should have introduced them already, but she could imagine he would probably prefer for her to take the initiative at this point. After all, he'd made it clear he didn't want to be too bothered with the details… Midnight phone calls notwithstanding.

'Imelda and Donal live on Donal's farm not ten minutes' drive away. If they can see you once you've had your lunch, I could get the groundskeeper to arrange a car for you to use?' said the ever-helpful Maureen.

'That would be wonderful,' Katie said, already excited about meeting Conall's sister. And perhaps not entirely for professional reasons.

During the tour of the grounds earlier, the chatty Maureen had turned out to be a font of knowledge on the O'Riordan family's affairs, nattering away about the details of Conall's and his sisters' upbringing which had brought back the soft glow Katie had felt yesterday for her new client.

Apparently Conall and his two younger sisters—Carmel and Imelda—were extremely close. Their father had died when Conall was only sixteen and the girls much younger, and then their mother had passed away two years later. But, instead of allowing his sisters to be taken in by distant relatives or fostered out, he'd instead insisted on becoming their legal guardian while having to run the family farm single-handed.

She had a much harder time imagining the man she had met being a surrogate father to two little girls than she did imagining him managing to found and grow a billion-dollar agricultural empire.

It was a feat she couldn't help being extremely impressed by when she considered her own family's hopelessly dysfunctional past. If you could even call her and Ross a family anymore. She had to take her hat off to Conall, too, for not abandoning his sister when she had chosen to marry her childhood sweetheart against his wishes.

Meeting Imelda O'Riordan would give her an insight into Conall's softer side, a softer side he kept well hidden in business and which—as much as she knew she shouldn't—Katie had to admit she was intrigued to discover more about. A lot more.

'I'm sorry, who are you now?' Imelda O'Riordan's striking blue eyes, so like her brother's, narrowed as her gaze fixed on Katie's face.

Conall's sister slapped the haunch of a horse

whose hooves she had been checking over when Katie had entered the barn and strode out of the stall, staring at Katie as if she had two heads. Lean and tall, with flowing black hair ruthlessly tied back in a serviceable ponytail, and wearing worn jeans and an old T-shirt splattered with mud, Imelda O'Riordan had the same stunning colouring—and intimidating stare—as her brother.

The frown on her brow was remarkably familiar too.

'My name's Katherine Hamilton,' Katie began. 'Maureen said she spoke to you about me popping over to discuss your plans for the wedding?' she finished, feeling almost as tongue-tied as she had with Conall yesterday. What was it about the O'Riordan siblings? Did intimidating frowns run in the family?

Imelda's brow puckered even more as she gave Katie a searching once over. 'Uh-huh, but no way are you from Flaherty's. Paddy's far too tight to employ someone as fancy as you.'

'Flaherty's?' It was Katie's turn to frown, Imelda's tone had made the 'fancy' comment sound like code for 'stuck up'. 'I'm sorry, I don't…' she began.

'Flaherty's Pub in Westport,' the other woman said, removing the gloves she wore and tucking them into the back pocket of her jeans. 'The place Donal and I hired for our wedding.'

What the...? Katie swallowed, feeling sick as she gripped the folder of concepts she had under her arm.

Had Conall intended the lavish wedding at Kildaragh as a surprise for his sister and her intended? She'd never heard of anyone throwing a surprise wedding before, but perhaps it was an Irish thing. And now she'd put her foot in it and ruined his surprise. But, really, why hadn't he told her?

'I'm so sorry. I think there may have been a mistake.' She turned, stifling the urge to wring her new client's neck as she shot out of the barn. All she could do now was damage limitation until she found out exactly what was going on.

'Hey, wait up.' Imelda, with her much longer legs, caught up with her in a few strides and grasped her elbow to halt her speedy exit. 'You still haven't told me who you are.'

She jerked Katie to a stop so fast, the folder flew out of her hands.

Katie swore as her sketches, suppliers' brochures, photos and samples scattered across the muddy floor like so much confetti. She had everything backed up on her laptop, but even so, she was supposed to be showing this to Conall in an hour's time. And now it was covered in… Was that even mud? Because it didn't smell like mud…

'Really, I'm nobody,' she said, dropping to her knees. 'I shouldn't have come over like this…' She scrambled to gather up the papers, racking her brains to think of how to explain her presence to Imelda—and how she was going to explain the horse manure all over her work to Conall.

But then Imelda knelt beside her and picked up one of the sketches Katie had done of a possible mediaeval Irish theme, complete with fabric swatches and colour schemes to go with the castle's early history.

'This looks glorious,' Imelda murmured, the awe in her voice bringing Katie's frantic movements to an abrupt stop. 'And this,' she said, picking up another sketch which Katie had developed, centred around the local myths and folklore.

Katie managed to take a breath. 'Thank you,' she said as she lifted the two designs from Imelda's fingers.

'You're a wedding planner!' Imelda declared. 'A really grand one!'

Katie nodded, because what else could she do? She was totally busted. 'I'm an event planner. I…'

'Conall hired you, didn't he? To work on a wedding for me at Kildaragh?'

Katie sunk back on her haunches, dumping the last of the muddy paperwork back in the folder as the young woman's astute gaze fixed on her face. *Oh, damn.* She'd really messed up. 'Yes, although I suspect he'll *definitely* want to fire me now that I've totally ruined his surprise.'

'That sneaky, high-handed bastard,' Imelda declared, but her lips had lifted into a cheeky grin that made her look even more beautiful. Clearly devastating dimples ran in the O'Riordan family, too. 'Surprise my bum,' she added, her true-blue eyes sparking with mischief.

'I'm sorry, I don't understand…' Katie began, struggling to get a grip on the conversation now. She knew she'd screwed up and her big commission was about to sink into the horse manure with her sketches. No way was O'Riordan going to put up with an error of this magnitude after giving her so much grief for being two and a half minutes late. But why his sister found the whole situation so amusing, she had no clue.

'Don't be sorry,' Imelda said. 'This is absolutely not your fault. This is my brother messing with me. Or you. Or possibly the both of us,' she said. 'I have no idea what his game is here—because he's made no bones about trying everything in his power to stop this wedding—but he's up to something. I'm sure of it…'

'Perhaps he's changed his mind?' Katie offered, finally getting a grip on the conversation, but still not sure what was going on.

'Have you met my brother?' Imelda asked, giving Katie a pitying look.

'Yes,' Katie said, mortified when her mind chose that precise moment to replay an image of Conall O'Riordan demanding things of her in last night's dreams that had nothing whatsoever to do with event planning… Her cheeks ignited.

'Then you know what a cynical, controlling, sneaky bastard he is,' Imelda supplied, apparently not having noticed Katie's flaming complexion.

Thank goodness for the barn's low lighting or this would be even more excruciating.

'Well, he…' Katie hesitated. She didn't want to agree with Imelda, because that would be totally unprofessional. Conall O'Riordan was a client—or possibly an ex-client—but she couldn't quite bring herself to disagree with his sister's caustic assessment of her brother's character because… Well, he had been quite a pill last night and during their interview a week ago.

'He can be quite a demanding employer,' she managed. 'That's true.'

'Demanding is one way of putting it,' Imelda announced with a full-bodied laugh—part-scoff, part-snort. 'Put it this way,' Imelda continued, 'With Conall, there's always an ulterior motive.

A hidden agenda. Some underhanded scheme to bend people to his will. And his will, last time I looked, was to oppose my marriage to Donal with every fibre of his being, because apparently only another gazillionaire will ever be good enough for his baby sister.'

Imelda scoff-snorted again, obviously as unimpressed with Conall's opinion of her choice of husband as Katie had once been with her brother Ross's opinion of Tom. 'So, if he's got you designing a wedding for me…' She lifted the grubby sketches back up. 'A really spectacular wedding, by the way, then he's doing it for a reason that has nothing whatsoever to do with actually giving me a wedding day to remember.'

'But are you sure he isn't doing it because he loves you?' Katie said, not quite able to let go of the conviction that behind Conall's taciturn, dictatorial, overbearing façade was a big softie just waiting to get out.

Oh, pur-lease... Is that for real, what you think, or is it just your hormones playing 'justify the inappropriate attraction'?

'Ah, sure, he loves me.' Imelda interrupted Katie's thoughts, her tone suggesting her brother's love was more of a burden than a benefit. 'But he also thinks he's the boss of everyone, especially me, and Carmel and even Mac. And your little man is only three!'

Your little man? Who is Mac? Does Conall O'Riordan have a child? A child he hasn't thought to mention?

Disgust had Katie's heartbeat galloping into her throat—and her sympathy drying up fast.

Her father had always refused to acknowledge her. She'd been the daughter of one of his mistresses, a 'by-blow', a 'bastard', a 'mistake'—all names she'd been called by the snooty kids in the boarding school Ross had insisted on sending her to after her mother's death.

At least Ross had acknowledged her as soon as he'd found out about her existence when her mother's solicitor had contacted him. How pathetically grateful she'd been for that when she'd been fourteen and alone. Until he'd decided to 'un-acknowledge' her five years later.

But it had never been Ross's job to recognise her. It had been Aldous De Courtney's, and he never had.

Was Conall a man much worse than her brother? A man like her father? Not just arrogant and cynical, but selfish and cold?

'Take it from me, Conall never does anything out of the goodness of his heart,' Imelda said, riding roughshod over Katie's latest internal monologue. 'Mostly because he doesn't have much of a heart. He's like the Grinch… It shrank after Daddy's death, and then again after Mammy's, and then again and again the richer and more powerful he became. Until finally it became almost invisible when Carmel got pregnant with Little Mac and wouldn't tell him who the father was.'

Little Mac is Conall's nephew—and someone else he feels responsible for.

'I see,' Katie said, the wave of relief that she hadn't completely misjudged her client followed by a wave of sadness, for Conall O'Riordan and his shrunken heart—even though she was well aware he would hate her pity as much as her lack of punctuality.

But is his heart really shrunken, or is it just guarded? The way any heart would become after too much tragedy? And so much responsibility?

'Ha, I think I've got it!' Imelda announced, dragging Katie back to reality and the problem at hand. Instead of the one in her overactive imagination.

Why on earth was she concerning herself with the workings of Conall O'Riordan's heart? When it would be much more productive to concern herself with how she was going to keep this commission?

'Got what, exactly?' Katie asked as politely as possible, as she noticed how Imelda's eyes had narrowed on her face.

'Con's ulterior motive for employing you to plan me a fancy wedding,' Imelda supplied patiently, as if Katie were ever so slightly stupid. 'Which he probably has no intention of following through on because he doesn't want me and Donal to get hitched.'

'Which is?' Katie asked, intrigued now by the mischievous spark in Imelda's blue eyes. After the comprehensive briefing she'd had from Maureen earlier, on the complete history of the O'Riordan siblings, she knew Imelda was twenty-one, three years younger than her, but she could suddenly imagine Conall's sister as a child who had probably run her brother ragged.

'You!' Imelda announced as if she had just solved the crime of the century.

'I beg your pardon?' Katie said, wary now, as well as confused. Had Imelda figured out that Katie had never quite been able to keep a professional perspective where her new client was concerned? Her already vibrant cheeks warmed even more at the compromising prospect. She'd always been accused of being too transparent, but this was becoming seriously awkward.

'You.' Imelda pointed at Katie and laughed. 'You're the reason he's organising a wedding for me. You're really pretty and super cute and—from those sketches—obviously brilliant.'

'Well, thank you… I think,' Katie replied, not sure whether she was being complimented or insulted now, because…um… *Cute?* Who wanted to be called cute? Especially by a woman as stunning as Conall's sister? And where on earth was Imelda's pseudo-compliment leading? Because Katie was already getting a bad feeling about the knowing look in the other woman's eyes.

'You're welcome,' Imelda said without breaking stride. 'And, the biggest clue of all, Conall dumped his last mistress—Christy Cavanagh—a few months ago, when Christy started making noises about marriage.'

'You've lost me,' Katie said, humiliated by the ridiculous spike of jealousy when she recalled the striking supermodel she had seen in several of the photos she'd found of Conall O'Riordan on the internet while prepping for their first interview.

'Isn't it obvious he wants to date you?'

'He...? *Wh-a-a-at?*' The last of Katie's cool deserted her. Was Conall's sister actually serious? And where on earth had that spurt of excitement come from at the thought that Conall O'Riordan—the scarily hot and super-dominant and overwhelming man she'd shared a difficult interview, one tense helicopter ride and a few wildly inappropriate wet dreams with—would be interested in *her*, in anything other than a professional capacity?

Forget wildly inappropriate. She'd just shot straight to insane without passing Go.

'Conall. He's planning to hit on you. That must be why he's hired you,' Imelda said, repeating her insane theory and making Katie's pulse rate hit the stratosphere.

'But that's…' *Pretty creepy, actually.* The truth was, if Imelda were right, she totally ought to be insulted and not at all impressed or giddy.

No matter how drop-dead gorgeous Conall O'Riordan was, men who hired women because they wanted to sleep with them were basically creeps, whatever way you looked at it. She ought to know, after all—wasn't that how her father had met her mother? By hiring her to renovate a fresco at a *palazzo* he owned in Rome while she was backpacking through Europe after finishing art school. Then he'd seduced her, keeping her as his mistress for months while insisting he loved her, before dumping her as soon as she'd become pregnant with Katie.

'Does he usually date women who work for him?' she asked, trying to get her heartbeat under control and figure out exactly how freaked out she should be about Conall's motives—not to mention her insane reaction to them.

'No, never.' Imelda's brow creased, as if she were reconsidering her theory. 'Fair point. He's kind of a stickler for stuff like that. But there's always a first time… And Con never goes more than a few weeks without a woman, and it's been over two months since he dumped Christy, so there's that,' Imelda added, warming to her theme again. 'Plus, since he became a billionaire, women tend to chase him instead of the other way around, and he hates that. Did I mention he's a control freak?'

'Yes, you did,' Katie said, starting to realise she was getting way too much information about her client's dating habits from his little sister. And it wasn't helping to calm down her giddy pulse one bit.

'Really, Imelda, I think you're totally wrong about this. Your brother is definitely not interested in me in anything other than a professional capacity,' she said, deciding an intervention was called for, before this conversation got any more out of hand. And/or she had a heart attack. 'And I'm also not remotely interested in him,' she said firmly.

Surely she couldn't be held responsible for a few inappropriate sensations and one night of wayward dreams? She was under pressure and she'd never... Well, she'd never met a man quite like Conall O'Riordan before. As much as she had adored Tom, they had always been far too comfortable to create the kind of sparks that Conall O'Riordan clearly inspired in every woman he encountered. The man oozed testosterone. And she was obviously way more susceptible to that hormonal call to arms than she had ever realised.

She refused to feel guilty about it though. Or freaked out… *Much*.

It was a sign, that was all, that her body was finally ready to come out of hibernation. Numbness had been her friend for the year of Tom's illness… And the years after his death. It had helped her to deal with her grief and her anger, and eventually helped her channel what had once been her love for Tom into her love for her work. It had allowed her to concentrate on the important things in life. But she couldn't be numb for ever. Just because Conall O'Riordan—or rather her reaction to him—had made her realise that, didn't mean this physical yearning had any other significance. And it certainly did not mean she needed to act on it, or to get too hung up on Imelda O'Riordan's insane theories about her brother's dating intentions.

'But don't you see that makes you the perfect candidate?' Imelda said, still flogging her dead theory.

Katie glanced at her watch pointedly, and rose to her feet, still shaky but a little less freaked out. 'I should go. I have an appointment with your brother at five back at the castle.'

An appointment she was looking forward to even less now. Not only did she have to explain to her client she'd told his sister about his plans—and deal with the possible fall out from that, because he had obviously intended to keep it a secret for some reason. But now she would have Imelda's mad theory in the back of her mind, which she suspected was not going to help her deal with the hormonal overload Conall O'Riordan inspired just by looking at her. And that was before she even factored in showing him the portfolio that she'd been waiting to wow him with for over a week, which was now covered in horse dung.

She brushed her hair back from her face, then tried to brush the mud off her jeans. *Terrific.* She didn't have time to change into the more professional outfit she had planned to wear for their meeting, because one thing she absolutely refused to be was late… Again.

'I'm really sorry to have bothered you and created a problem between you and your brother,' she said carefully to Imelda.

'What problem?' Imelda asked, looking nonplussed.

But Katie chose not to elaborate—and point out all the things Imelda had said were wrong with her older brother. She'd crossed about a hundred lines by coming here already. That would teach her not to act on her instincts and indulge her curiosity.

She reached out a hand. 'I really hope we get to work together on your wedding. I think Hamilton Events could do an amazing job for you and Donal and Mr O'Riordan.'

'Oh, I'm sure you could. Your designs are glorious. I love them,' Imelda said, taking Katie's hand and giving it a firm shake. 'And with Con footing the bill, it'll be so much grander than what we had planned at Flaherty's.'

The unguarded and effusive praise lifted Katie's spirits a little. Perhaps she could still salvage this job, if she worked her socks off and Conall never discovered exactly how personal her conversation with his sister had become. Because she had a sneaking suspicion that if he ever found *that* out he would have even more cause to fire her on the spot. And frankly she wouldn't blame him.

'I *am* the bride,' Imelda said. 'And, even though my opinion won't matter to my arrogant, control-freak brother, when you speak to him tell him I think the fairy theme is the best,' Imelda added, finally letting go of Katie's hand. 'And that he should definitely dress as a leprechaun to give me away.'

Katie opened her mouth to say she hadn't intended to include leprechauns in the theme. She was going for classy and mythical, not clichéd and crass—but then she spotted the mischievous twinkle in Imelda's eyes.

A laugh bubbled to her lips. 'That's not remotely funny. He'd definitely fire me if I suggested that!'

Imelda laughed too, and Katie realised that somehow or other, during their very short acquaintance, she'd made a friend. And that she really liked Conall's sister. Having never had a sister, but always having wanted one, it was a good feeling—even if this friendship turned out to be very short lived.

'Ah, go on now, I was only messing with you,' Imelda said, slapping Katie on the back in what she was beginning to realise was a typically easy-going gesture.

As Katie made her way back to the car she had borrowed from the Castle and climbed in with her muddy folder, she wondered how it was that Conall's sister was such an impetuous and enthusiastic sort when her brother was so guarded and cynical.

But then she remembered the details of their past. Imelda and her sister Carmel had been orphaned when they were only six and eight respectively, according to Maureen. And then Conall had become their guardian. So the way Imelda had turned out would be largely down to Conall's influence. Whatever friction there was now between the two siblings, Conall must have been a wonderful surrogate parent, no matter how over-protective and controlling, for his sister to be so confident and well-adjusted after losing both her parents when she was so young.

Imelda now stood at the threshold of the farmhouse beside her fiancé Donal, who had his arm slung around her waist. A strapping young farmer, whom Katie had met earlier before being directed out to the barn, Donal Delaney obviously adored his bride-to-be.

Imelda waved goodbye as Katie backed the vehicle out of the yard. 'Good luck with Con, Ms Hamilton,' Imelda shouted after her. 'Even though I'm guessing you won't need it, because he's totally planning to hit on you—take my word for it.'

No, he's absolutely not. And I so don't want him to.

Katie frowned, attempting to concentrate on negotiating the rocky road in the late afternoon sunlight, rather than the wayward thoughts conjured up by Imelda's cheeky parting comment.

But as the castle came into view—gilded in reds and golds as the sun started to sink into the Atlantic behind it—her heartbeat kicked back up to warp speed and a hot weight swelled between her thighs.

Gee, thanks, Imelda.

CHAPTER FOUR

Good luck with the new romance, big bro! FINALLY you've found someone to hit on who isn't a sour-faced stick insect. I approve—&, btw, thx for seeing the light & offering to bankroll a fancy wedding for me and Donal at Kildaragh. I love your girl's ideas—at least as much as I love you. We accept! Immy x

CONALL STARED AT the text from his sister that had just popped up on his phone and tried to make head or tail of it.

New romance? Your girl? *What* girl? And how had she got wind of the wedding planning?

Imelda had taken great joy in messing with him ever since she'd been six years old and had realised how far out of his depth her big brother was trying to be both father and mother to two little girls. He'd had to learn everything from scratch, and fast—from how to plait an eight-year-old's hair at seven in the morning, when you'd already been up for three hours milking cows, to how to deal with night terrors and bed-wetting when you were cross-eyed with exhaustion and grief-stricken too. Imelda, with her eagle-eyed attention to detail, had spotted all his failings, pointed them out at great length and then told him how to fix them.

But she hadn't messed with him in a while. In fact, they'd hardly been speaking—ever since their latest falling out over her decision to marry Donal Delaney. Donal was a nice enough lad, but nowhere near good enough for her. And did she really want to be some man's wife for the rest of her life when Conall had been grooming her to take over O'Riordan's Irish division ever since she'd graduated from Trinity this summer with a first in Agricultural Science?

Of course, even when she wasn't speaking to him, Imelda usually had a lot to say about his choice of girlfriend. Both his sisters did. But where had she got the idea he needed her approval to date anyone? And who the heck was she talking about? He didn't do romance and he hadn't yet had time—or frankly the inclination—to find a replacement for Christy after their bust-up. He hadn't meant to hurt her, but when had he ever given her the impression he was interested in more than superficial sex and entertaining company?

'Conall, Miss Hamilton has just arrived for her five o'clock appointment.'

He looked up from his phone to see his assistant step aside and the woman who had crowded into far too many of his thoughts appear in the doorway.

He tensed against the now familiar ripple of awareness. He was annoyed when he noticed the way the casual outfit of jeans and a soft sweater hugged her voluptuous curves—and the ripple turned into a definite jolt.

He stood and tucked the phone into his back pocket. Whatever Imelda's game was, he would have to deal with it later, because he had a more pressing problem. Somehow his sister had found out he'd hired a wedding planner, and now she was expecting him to follow through on hosting an event at Kildaragh he didn't even agree with, when he hadn't yet made a definite decision about it.

But the way she had finished the message had got to him.

Immy.

It was the nickname he'd given her when she'd been a baby, a nickname he hadn't used since their mammy's funeral, when she'd looked up at him with a solemn tear-streaked face and announced she was 'too grown up' for silly nicknames.

The wave of emotion at seeing that nickname again was something he liked even less than the arousal still charging through his body, because it was going to force him to rethink his strategy and host this damn wedding after all. And that meant working with this woman for a lot longer than a week. A woman whom he didn't want to notice, let alone be attracted to, but somehow was.

'Hello, Mr O'Riordan, I hope I'm not late?' Katherine Hamilton said as she walked into the room and sent him a tentative smile that still somehow managed to light up her heart-shaped face.

The comment seemed guileless, but he had to wonder if she too was messing with him now.

If she was, it was a mistake, because he did not take kindly to having the mickey taken out of him. And, frankly, he was already on edge enough after Imelda's cryptic text not to appreciate the dig at his surly behaviour yesterday before their flight.

He glanced at his watch. 'No, you're not late this time,' he said bluntly, being sure that he did not react to the smile—which even more annoyingly made her cheeks glow with a becoming flush.

Her make-up had been immaculate the day before and during their interview a week ago—but this afternoon she did not appear to be wearing any. For the first time, he noticed the sprinkle of freckles scattered across her nose. The tiny blemishes on her clear dewy skin, coupled with the dishevelled casual clothing—was that mud on her jeans?—and the eager smile made her seem even younger and hotter than she'd been during last night's helicopter trip.

The blood pounded beneath his belt on cue and he straightened.

Don't be a sap. She's not sweet, or innocent. How can she be if she's a De Courtney? This is desire plain and simple—and the emotional side-swipe of having Imelda use her old nickname.

'Sit down,' he said, indicating the seat in front of his desk, before he sat behind it, determined not to lose sight of his motivations for bringing Katherine Hamilton to Kildaragh.

He wanted to find out more about her brother. And maybe part of him also wanted to punish her for being a De Courtney, for having all the privileges and opportunities his own sister Carmel had been denied when she'd had a child at nineteen. Just because he might have to go through with Imelda's wedding at Kildaragh now, didn't mean he couldn't still put Katherine Hamilton through her paces while he was employing her.

He certainly didn't intend to make this commission easy for her. She didn't deserve easy.

She'd had enough easy in her life already, while her brother had ensured that Carmel's life was far too hard.

He gave her far-too-hot jeans-and-sweater combo a scathing once-over, making sure she knew he was not impressed with the informality of her appearance—even if his groin was giving it a round of applause.

'I'm sorry for the casual attire.' She gave a nervous huff. 'I didn't have time to change into something more suitable,' she added, her cheeks igniting. 'I've been so busy today, checking out the castle. I wanted to get a head start on all the logistics, working out a schedule for the events, planning possible venues for the different activities…'

He interrupted her babble. 'Next time find the time to dress appropriately.' Had he flustered her? *Good.*

'Okay,' she said, the obedience in her tone somewhat contradicted by the flash of something provocative in her eyes. Indignation, irritation, rebellion? Whatever it was, that flash had made his groin pulse harder.

Then she hooked the wild hair behind her ear and he caught a tantalising whiff of her delicious scent—orange and rosemary—which had intoxicated him on the chopper ride. And he had to bite his tongue to stop himself from drawing in a greedy lungful.

Good God, what was wrong with him? This woman was the privileged, pampered sister of a man he despised. A man who had wronged *his* sister and abandoned his own child.

How could he feel anything for her but disgust?

'Did you bring the portfolio with you?' he asked, suddenly keen to get this meeting over with and her out of his personal space, until he'd got this unfortunate reaction under control. And figured out what exactly he was going to do about her, his sister's wedding and Imelda's typically confusing text.

That was all this was—Imelda had unsettled him with that text, and it was impacting his ability to control his unwanted attraction to Katherine Hamilton.

'Um...no,' she said, taking the laptop she had under her arm and flipping it open.

But, as she placed the laptop on his desk and clicked the power button, heat rose up her neck—giving her dewy skin a pink glow.

What was that about? What had she done to feel guilty about? Because he would recognise a guilty flush like that from thirty paces. After all, he'd been the legal guardian of two teenage girls for nine never-ending years.

'I thought I'd show you my ideas on the laptop…' she began, her gaze fixed firmly on the computer screen as she opened a series of files and documents.

'What happened to the portfolio?' he asked. Why was she avoiding eye contact?

The guilty flush exploded in her cheeks as her gaze darted to his. Not just guilt. What he saw also looked like a compelling combination of shame and maybe even panic. Katherine Hamilton was nothing if not completely transparent.

'It got a little muddy,' she said.

'How? And where?' he asked as the pieces suddenly began to slot into place.

The new romance? Your girl's ideas? There was only one new person on the estate at the moment. Only one person he had brought with him from London. And only one person who was likely to have shown Imelda the ideas for the wedding and told her about his plans to use Kildaragh Castle.

Katherine Hamilton had spoken to his sister, had pitched her ideas to her, without asking him first.

How dared she take such a liberty?

Fury flooded through his system, exacerbated by the sharp stab of desire that arrowed down when she licked her lips—the guilt and panic in her gaze like that of a doe who had just spotted the hunter. Why that should make the pulsing in his groin start to pound only made him more furious.

'Did you speak to Imelda,' he asked, because she hadn't replied, 'without my permission?'

You have really blown it this time, Katie.

Conall O'Riordan looked really mad. And utterly magnificent.

For goodness' sake, Katie. Mad and magnificent do not go together, at all.

'Yes, I'm afraid I did. I went to the Delaney farm this afternoon,' she rushed to continue as his steely frown became catastrophic and the twitching muscle in his jaw hardened. 'I just wanted to meet her. To pass a few of my ideas for the themes by her, before consulting with you. It seemed appropriate, as she's the bride. I had no idea the wedding was supposed to be a surprise.'

'It's not supposed to be a surprise.'

Then why are you so mad?

'I see, well, it's definitely not one now,' Katie replied, desperately trying to sound upbeat and not apologetic or flustered, even though her pulse rate had hit the stratosphere. 'But the good news is Imelda loved some of the ideas. She's particularly keen on the myths and folklore theme.'

'Oh, is she, now?' he snarled. He literally

snarled, still glaring at her with those deep-blue eyes as if she'd just shot his dog or something.

She didn't get it. Why was he so furious? And how could that frigid gaze feel as if it were incinerating every inch of exposed skin when it was so chillingly disapproving?

The unsettling reaction forced her to breathe and regroup…as she frantically tried to figure out what on earth was going on. Conall O'Riordan had been obstructive and unforthcoming about every detail of this commission so far. He'd put her off, treated her with disdain and got worked up about what were ultimately fairly minor issues.

Normally she would avoid conflict. She was not the sort of person who thrived on confrontation—she worked in events, for goodness' sake. But she'd dealt with arrogant, overbearing men before, Ross being a case in point, and she happened to know that giving ground when they had effectively backed you into a corner was not a good strategy.

If she'd allowed herself to be bullied by Ross, she never would have had those few precious days as Tom's wife. She would never regret those moments, even though it had cost her dearly in terms of her relationship with her brother. And, while she desperately wanted this commission, she could not do it with any degree of success if she couldn't communicate with Conall O'Riordan honestly and openly.

Taking a deep breath, she gathered every ounce of courage she had, determined to stand up to him. 'If the wedding's not a surprise for Imelda, why is it a problem that I consulted her?' she asked, pleased when her voice sounded clear and direct—despite the ball of nerves tying her stomach in a knot.

If Imelda was right, and Conall O'Riordan had some ulterior motive for hiring her, she needed to know what it was. Because even thinking it might be the one Imelda had suggested was making her panic and her anxiety increase, along with those unwanted jolts of sensation that had plagued her whenever she was within two feet of this man. And she could see the fire in his eyes or smell the enticing scent of clean pine soap and spicy juniper-berry cologne.

She held her breath, trying to resist breathing in the intoxicating aroma, and braced herself, ready to be fired on the spot.

His brows lowered even further, his gaze so sharp now she was surprised it didn't slice through the last of her composure, the only sound in the room her breathing and his.

The stand-off seemed to last for several eternities, the silence stretching tight as the spark of something real and vivid sizzled over her skin.

She had no idea what that something was, but her body felt as if it were about to burst into flames as his gaze raked over her. Her staggered breathing slowed, her heart pounding painfully in her chest. The tight feeling in her ribs becoming as addictive as it was terrifying.

Then he broke eye contact.

Her breath released in a rush. And her stomach flipped over, the roar of triumph in her soul as unmistakeable as if she had faced down a dragon—an extremely hot dragon—and won.

Two heartbeats later, his gaze met hers again but, while his expression was still intense, still disturbing, he no longer looked as if he was about to explode.

'My sister and I don't always see eye to eye. She's passionate and tough, but also impulsive and reckless, and she likes to make my life hell on a regular basis, so I prefer to manage her involvement,' he said, so carefully she knew she wasn't getting the whole story. But this at least was a start, a basis for communication rather than conflict.

And, to be fair, he had a point about his sister. As much as she had enjoyed meeting Imelda, the woman was almost as much of a force of nature as her brother.

'I'm really not here to create difficulties between you and your sister,' she said, trying to be as conciliatory as possible now. He hadn't fired her. She could still do this wedding. But she needed to be one hundred per cent professional now.

Somehow she'd already crossed a line with Conall O'Riordan. A line that kept shifting and changing in ways she didn't really understand because, even though she was officially a widow, she had never had to deal with this level of physical attraction before. An attraction that was not just electrifying but volatile. The only way forward now was to establish boundaries, for her own protection.

'I'm just here to plan a wedding, but Imelda *is* the bride, so I think it's vitally important I consult with her as well as you.'

He continued to stare, his gaze seeming to peer into her soul, as if he could see things she had never known were there. But then he nodded, the movement stiff and forced, but enough of a concession to make Katie's heartbeat hit double time.

'Point taken,' he murmured. 'You can consult with her on all the details.' He indicated the laptop. 'In fact, you might as well put that away. You can show those files to her and Donal for approval.'

'Okay, good,' she murmured, closing her laptop and tucking it back under her arm, a little deflated at the realisation she would not be consulting with Conall O'Riordan in future—which made no sense at all, because consulting with him so far hadn't exactly been a picnic.

'Work with her this week, and once you've agreed everything give me a rundown of the costs involved,' he said.

'Absolutely. I'll make sure we stick closely to the budget you outlined,' she said.

His brow creased. 'The budget isn't an issue. I want her to be happy, even if she is determined to waste a perfectly good education,' he said, the brittle edge still there but blunted with resignation. 'If the costs go above the budget, just let me know.'

Katie nodded. She needed to leave now. His disagreements with Imelda over her marriage were none of her business. But, as she turned to go, she heard the sigh behind her—frustrated and weary—and she couldn't stop herself from turning back.

'For what it's worth, I think you're doing a wonderful thing, Mr O'Riordan,' she said. 'And that you're a really incredible brother.'

One sceptical eyebrow arched and that hot gaze sharpened again. 'Why?' The cynical tone was back with a vengeance. 'Because I'm willing to spend a fortune on a wedding that could quite probably ruin my sister's life?'

'No,' she said, absorbing the caustic comment and the implied criticism of what she did for a living, convinced his frustration wasn't directed at her. 'Because you're willing to support her choices, even though you don't agree with them. That's huge, and much rarer than you might think.'

He blinked, and she realised she had surprised him with her compliment. She wondered why.

'Maureen told me about how you became your sisters' guardian when you were little more than a boy yourself,' she continued, suddenly wanting to explain, even if it meant dancing over that line again. Maybe she wouldn't be working that closely with him, but if she couldn't get him on board with the wedding plans at least she might be able to make him less hostile to them…and her.

'Maureen told me how you brought them both up while working your family's farm and eventually building your business. It's obvious that you love them, and that Imelda loves you back, even if she does enjoy making your life hell.'

She wound to a stop, because he was now staring at her blankly, as if she'd completely lost her marbles. Maybe she had. The swell of emotion in her chest was choking off her air supply.

'Mrs Doolan talks too much,' he said, but the

muscle in his jaw had stopped twitching. What she saw in his eyes wasn't cynicism and impatience any more, it was rich and intense—and not entirely disapproving, giving her the courage to finish what she'd started.

'What I'm trying to say is that Imelda's confidence and determination and independence are all a testament to the sacrifices you made. She's her own woman, and that's down to you.'

'Exactly—I've created a monster,' he murmured, but his lips quirked in that almost-smile that told her, while he probably still wasn't happy about the wedding, he wasn't entirely opposed to it.

My work here is done.

But what should have given her relief gave her anything but when he continued to stare at her with that raptor-like focus, as if he were trying to look past the professional to something a great deal more personal.

'We can meet at the end of the week to go over the budget,' he said, his tone curt and businesslike, but his eyes continue to study her...making her far too aware of the sensations still rippling over her skin. 'Work out the event details with Imelda and Donal. I have a few people I should include on the guest list, but otherwise that can be Immy's domain.'

'Who's Immy?' she asked before she realised it must be Imelda. To her astonishment, he tensed at the innocuous question, and colour slashed across his tanned cheeks.

He cleared his throat. 'Imelda,' he said, his voice gruff. 'It's a nickname.'

His gaze slid away from hers at last. But Katie's heart skipped several beats as she watched his reaction to the unintentional slip.

No one could ever describe Conall O'Riordan as sweet. He was forceful, demanding, taciturn, supremely cynical and he did not suffer fools gladly. She'd certainly experienced how overbearing and uncompromising he could be after working for him for little more than a week. But in that moment, as she realised how uncomfortable he was at having her witness the unguarded use of his sister's pet name, she couldn't help being deeply touched. He might want to be a hard ass, might want to believe he could control every emotion and bend it to his will, but even he couldn't do that all the time.

He's human, even if he doesn't want to be.

The tender thoughts were quickly dispelled, though, when his harsh blue gaze locked back on her face.

The whisper of arousal arrowed down through her abdomen and became a roar.

'You can see yourself out, Ms Hamilton,' he said, the abrupt dismissal bristling with frustration.

She nodded and left, rushing out of the room, all of a sudden stupidly glad she wouldn't have to spend too much time in his company going forward, as the heat pulsed in her sex and rose up her torso to hit her cheeks.

What just happened?

She shot up to her suite of rooms—knowing she was more than likely going to have another disturbed night's sleep. Because it felt as if she hadn't just stepped over the line this time, she'd crashed over it, and now she was in no man's land. Stuck in a territory which she had no idea whatsoever how to get out of again. The endorphins charging through her were completely out of control—all as a result of one harsh, uncompromising, assessing look that probably hadn't meant anything to Conall O'Riordan but meant far too much to her.

But, more than that, she felt an emotional connection to this man now that made no sense whatsoever.

Because somehow, during just one day in Kildaragh, thanks to Conall's talkative housekeeper, his indiscreet sister and his own unbidden reaction to a perfectly innocuous comment, she'd discovered things—intimate and inappropriate things—about this overwhelming man that didn't just captivate and excite her far too inexperienced body…but also her far too open and easily bruised heart.

CHAPTER FIVE

FOR WHAT IT'S WORTH, I think you're doing a wonderful thing, Mr O'Riordan. And that you're a really incredible brother.

Conall strode out of the churning surf onto the sandy beach of the private cove below the castle, the words Katherine Hamilton had spoken to him a week ago still bugging him.

Why couldn't he get her, and the expression on her face that day—earnest, compassionate, sincere—out of his head? Why should he care what she thought of him, or his family?

The rocky cliffs which hugged the headland and the winter wetsuit he wore provided some shelter from the rain and wind that had picked up since he'd entered the water twenty minutes ago, but not nearly enough to stop him shivering violently as he stripped off the clinging neoprene and grabbed his towel.

After drying off as quickly as possible, he

donned the sweats he'd left sheltered under the rocks—the now damp sweats.

Perhaps he should go for a run to work off some more of the energy still charging through his body—a by-product of thinking about the wedding planner? Which he seemed to be doing all the damn time.

But as a gust of wind laden with the cold, fine spray of the October drizzle brushed over his skin he decided against it. This was madness. Hypothermia was not the way to keep thoughts of her out of his head, and his pants. And, anyway, he had controlled it this long. Just about.

He'd all but been forced to abandon plans to quiz her about her brother after their incendiary showdown in his office, deciding that creating distance between them was more important. He'd been swimming in the cove every day of the last week to leash the hunger that had blindsided him during their last meeting. And invaded his dreams every night since. And most of his waking hours as well.

He'd kept himself busy and made a point of staying away from the parts of his home he knew she was using to prep for the wedding and hold meetings and brainstorming sessions with a host of local suppliers, artists, catering staff and craftspeople, making her vision for the event a reality.

But despite his best efforts he'd caught glimpses of her, and they had tortured him, keeping her front and centre in his thoughts when he didn't want her to be there.

Such as when he'd spotted her from the window of his suite on Tuesday morning as she'd chatted expansively to his head groundskeeper in the walled gardens below, and her short curls had whipped around her face in the autumn breeze.

Or as she'd scribbled in her ever-present sketch book when he wandered past the entrance to the banqueting hall yesterday afternoon. She hadn't spotted him, but he'd paused to watch her for one breathless moment until the sight of her small, white teeth chewing on her bottom lip had sent a shaft of desire through his system so sharp it had taken him most of the afternoon to get over it.

Of course, his efforts to forget her had not been helped one iota by the fact his housekeeper, his personal assistants and pretty much every other person that worked in Kildaragh kept informing him how much they enjoyed working with her—despite the scowl on his face every time her name was mentioned, which must have told them he had no desire to discuss her.

Even his sister had rung him several times to sing the woman's praises, so excited now about the prospect of the wedding they were planning together that she seemed to have completely forgotten she wasn't speaking to him. Either that or Imelda had somehow guessed the best way to rile him was to talk non-stop about the woman he'd made it perfectly clear he had no interest in whatsoever.

Except that isn't true. You do have an interest in her. A volatile, incessant interest in her which has only got worse over the last seven days, despite freezing your backside off each afternoon and becoming a prisoner in your own castle.

He slung the wet towel over his shoulders and scooped up the sandy wetsuit, then trudged up the beach towards the steps carved into the rock.

Avoidance wasn't working.

Even those fleeting glimpses only stoked the flames that had been torturing him ever since the afternoon in his office when he'd been furious with her—until the fury had turned into something wild, visceral and untamed. And so uncontrolled he'd let his guard drop, enough to blurt out that daft nickname, and have the things Katherine said about what he'd done for his sisters mean something.

He didn't need her approval, or her sympathy. He certainly didn't need to be captivated by the sincerity in those wide, slightly tilted emerald eyes—devoid of make-up and guile—or the sadness.

But somehow he had been. And now it wasn't

just this incessant hunger driving him nuts. It was the thought she wasn't who he had decided she was. That he'd made a mistake, and couldn't punish her for her brother's sins. No matter how much he might want to.

Because for that split second, when she'd spoken so compassionately about his sisters and him, he'd looked into her face and seen honesty and regret…and not the entitled carelessness he'd wanted to see.

And now he wanted to know why.

Why had she looked so sad in that moment?

Why had what he'd done for his sisters moved her so deeply?

And why the heck should it matter to him?

He'd resisted the urge to pull out the investigation report for six days. The one he'd commissioned four years ago when Carmel had run away from art college in London, pregnant, alone and devastated, refusing to name the father of her baby. The investigation that had finally led him to the man he was now convinced was Mac's father.

But, when he'd pulled out the report again last night, it had given him no more details than he already knew about Katherine Hamilton. Just her name, her business address and the fact that she was Ross De Courtney's only known blood relation. A half-sister who Conall had assumed the man must love very much, as he'd paid for her to go to an extremely exclusive boarding school—even though she was his father's illegitimate child.

But now he wasn't even sure about that.

You're willing to support her choices, even though you don't agree with them. That's huge, and much rarer than you might think.

Somehow those quietly spoken words—and the other things she'd said that afternoon—had pierced through the wall he kept around his heart.

A wall that he'd constructed brick by tortuous brick, ever since he'd walked into his mother's bedroom one Christmas morning thirteen years ago and found…

He cut off the cruel memory and smothered the wave of self-loathing which came with it.

Yeah, so not going there. Not when my mind is messed up enough already by this woman.

He made his way up the castle's back stairs to his suite of rooms in the east wing. After dumping the towel and wetsuit in the basket for the housekeeping staff, he stripped off the damp sweats then walked into the *en suite* bathroom and turned on the power shower.

He stepped under the needle-sharp spray and washed the salt and sand out of his hair and off his skin. Then he switched the dial down to frigid, to control the pulsing ache in his groin which was back, despite the freezing swim.

Grand, just what I need before I see her again.

He got dressed then checked the clock on his smart phone. He was late for their appointment. An appointment he'd considered cancelling a ton of times. He didn't really need to okay the wedding budget. He could easily pass that responsibility off to his financial director. But each time he'd contemplated cancelling he'd known he didn't want to… Because now, as well as the hunger, there was the curiosity, that nagging feeling that there was much more to Katherine Hamilton than he'd realised.

She was scheduled to leave Kildaragh tomorrow morning once they went over the budget—and he would have no need to see her again until the wedding itself in several weeks.

Which should have been a good thing. The perfect excuse to get her out of his mind, as well as his sight. But, try as he might, he couldn't deny the deep pulse of yearning. And the even more disturbing desire to know much more about her. He wanted to discover the secrets that lurked behind those guileless emerald eyes…

Surely this yearning was really just about him finishing what he had started by hiring her in the first place? he told himself. Nothing more, nothing less.

Had her brother let her down too? And, if he had, could Katherine Hamilton give him information he could use against Ross De Courtney if he needed to?

And if the hunger turned out to be mutual…? Would it really be so wrong to use it to get closer to her, for Carmel's sake? For Mac's?

He made his way back down the castle stairs towards his office in the east wing. So what if he wanted her? It could be useful, especially if she wanted him in return. She couldn't possibly be as innocent as that flush of awareness had suggested when he'd first met her. And she wouldn't get past his wall again, because he was ready for her now.

He thrust open the door to his office and she jumped up from her seat, her fingers wrapped around her laptop and her face a picture of surprise and… Was that pleasure?

Something surged up his torso…and he knew. This meeting didn't have to be an end, it could be a beginning.

An idea formed in his head as he recalled the ball at the Hotel de Lumière in Paris, which he was attending on Sunday night. He hadn't wanted to go to the event, as he usually hated those kind of dressy, pointlessly fancy affairs, but he'd been strong-armed into it by his PR team. Apparently it would help if he was a lot more visible in the

French media before they floated O'Riordan's European division on the Paris Stock Exchange in two weeks' time.

'Good afternoon, Ms Hamilton,' he said, spreading his arm out to indicate she sit down again. 'Take a seat.'

He marched round his desk but, as he watched her brush her pencil skirt over her bottom before taking her seat, and saw her blouse stretch over her breasts, the thought of seeing her in something glittering and a lot more revealing had the idea becoming fully formed.

Maybe it was impetuous, even a little reckless—which was not at all like him—but why not?

Katherine Hamilton was a romantic. She'd said it herself. And, while he'd doubted it at first, he had become convinced of it in the last week, after the way she had bonded so quickly with his love-struck sister. From the few glimpses he'd been given of the fanciful fairy-tale design they'd settled on together for the wedding, from that heartfelt look when she'd spoken of family and commitment and love, and from the flush warming her cheeks now.

He hadn't imagined the awareness in her eyes when she'd turned round a moment ago, either.

Why not give her a little of the romance she craved? And get them both what they wanted? Seducing more information about her brother out of her wouldn't be that hard. And they could both enjoy the results immensely, if the desire pumping through his veins was anything to go by.

She placed the laptop on the desk, powered it up and started talking about the budget she'd worked out for his sister's wedding in that business-like tone—somewhat belied by the vivid flush on her face and the rapid rise and fall of her breathing beneath her blouse. He asked what he hoped were pertinent questions, while considering how to invite her to Paris and get her to the ball without scaring her off.

Because he had the definite impression Katherine Hamilton found him intimidating as well as exciting.

He smiled, as on cue she bit into her bottom lip, while bringing up a spreadsheet of estimates from the local suppliers and contractors.

Intimidating is good, Con... All the better to sweep her off her feet with.

Keep talking, don't look at him and stop blushing, for Pete's sake.

'As you can see, we've managed to find a lot of really terrific and also cost-effective suppliers in Galway and Mayo. Imelda was particularly keen on sourcing locally and I agree with her.'

Katie took a much-needed breath, the figures on her spreadsheet starting to blur—probably from lack of oxygen. Why did she find it so hard to breathe when she was near him? And to remain professional? Perhaps it was the smile he'd treated her to when he'd walked into his office—as if he'd been genuinely pleased to see her—that had sucked all the air out of the room.

Or maybe it was the memory of him walking out of the surf half an hour ago, from her vantage point in her room as she prepared for this meeting, the contours of his muscular frame perfectly displayed in a leave-nothing-to-the-imagination wetsuit.

It was a guilty pleasure she'd got into the habit of indulging every day now, ever since she'd spotted him taking his swim on Sunday afternoon, and had discovered the next afternoon—when she'd just happened to be watching from her window again at precisely the same time—that it was something he scheduled every day at around four p.m.

A guilty pleasure she was now paying the price for, big time.

How was a woman supposed to concentrate on euros and cents and the intricacies of finding the perfect florist when all she could see was Conall O'Riordan's magnificent physique displayed in clinging wet neoprene as he battled the elements, and when all she could smell was the clean, spicy scent of soap and man?

She sucked in a breath and forced herself to conclude her presentation. 'So, as you can see, I've got some really competitive quotes and Imelda is very happy with the progress so far.'

'Grand, email the spreadsheet to my financial director.' The deep voice concluded, ending the presentation she'd been practising for over an hour—before she'd got distracted by the sight of him in a wetsuit, his dark hair plastered to his forehead, his muscular chest gilded with moisture as he'd stripped down to his…

Focus. On the work, not the six-pack reveal.

'Um…yes, of course,' she managed, forcing her gaze to his face and that far-too-knowing blue gaze.

Unfortunately, his features—and the cobalt blue of his irises—were no less breath-taking than the sight of his naked chest half an hour ago, now tattooed on her frontal lobe.

'I've given him the budget and you can liaise with him now about the details,' he added, his lips quirking in rueful amusement that had all her freak-out vibes freaking out more.

Did he know that she'd been spying on him every day at four? Could he see the compromising image inside her head—seared there for all eternity—of rippling abs, bulging biceps, the sprinkle of chest hair that arrowed down past his hip flexors to…

Stop! And say something... Preferably something relevant and coherent, if possible.

'Um...absolutely. *You* don't need me to email you my spreadsheet, then?' she asked.

One dark eyebrow arched, and his lips curled on one side—turning the rueful quirk into a definite smile. 'Your spreadsheet?' he said, the teasing tone doing diabolical things to the heat in her face, which chose that precise moment to start wending its way down her torso. 'No.' He paused, his amusement unmistakeable. 'Although your spreadsheet looks very...accomplished,' he finished, almost as if the word 'spreadsheet' were a euphemism for something else entirely.

'Thank you,' she said, not entirely sure what they were talking about any more, because it definitely didn't feel like spreadsheets. 'Well, I suppose...' She switched off her laptop, trying not to regret the fact their meeting was effectively over. 'I should go then, unless you had any other questions about the budget? Or the wedding plans?' she asked, trying not to wince when she heard the eagerness in her voice. Exactly how desperate was she to spend a few more precious minutes in his company?

'I don't have any other questions about the commission, no,' he said.

She nodded, not able to speak round the stupid regret now as she shoved her laptop back into her briefcase, keen to get out of his office before she did something really mortifying. Like beg… Or hyper-ventilate.

Seriously, Katie, haven't you already been unprofessional enough with your recently discovered Peeping Tom tendencies?

'But I do have another question that has nothing to do with the wedding.'

She looked up to see those intense blue eyes locked on her face. Her still burning face.

'Actually, it's more of a request than a question,' he said, his eyes darkening. 'I need a date for the Lumière Ball tomorrow night in Paris.'

'I'm sorry…what?' she asked sharply, so shocked she was fairly sure she must just have had an audio hallucination of some sort. Either that or she'd got totally the wrong end of the stick.

Had he just asked her on a date—to the Lumière Ball, the most prestigious and exclusive event in Europe's winter season? Only billionaires, movie stars, royalty and other assorted very, *very* important people attended the Lumière Ball.

But it wasn't really the thought of the ball—any event planner's dream to attend—that was giving her breathing difficulties. It was the thought of going with *him*. She blinked, struggling to shake the fanciful thought loose. No, it wasn't possible. She was his event planner. An event planner whom she wasn't even sure he really liked very much. She must have misunderstood him.

'I don't know anyone you could ask,' she said, wondering if perhaps he thought she ran an escort service on the side.

Asking her to find him a date was odd—especially as he was probably one of the world's most eligible bachelors, so must have a string of glamazons at his fingertips to call on at a moment's notice. But it was probably not the oddest request she'd ever had, if you included the septuagenarian couple who had asked her if they could celebrate their golden wedding anniversary by abseiling down Tower Bridge.

'Katherine…' he said, the lip quirk turning into another slow smile. 'Do you mind if I call you Katherine?' he asked, getting up to walk round his desk and perch on the corner of it—right in front of her.

'Katie,' she murmured. He was so close she could see the dimple in his cheek peeking from the five o'clock shadow. And the sparkle of amusement in his eyes—which reminded her of the sparkle in Imelda's eyes. Except not. Because Imelda's sparkle didn't give her goose bumps.

'Sorry?' he said.

'Katie.' She cleared her throat to stop her voice

from rising even more. 'People call me Katie. No one calls me Katherine.'

'That's a shame. Katherine suits you better,' he said. 'Katie sounds like a girl's name, instead of a woman's.'

'You can call me Katherine if you'd rather,' she replied, her voice so breathless now she was surprised she hadn't passed out.

'Good. So, just to be crystal-clear—it's you I'm asking on a date, Katherine. No one else.'

'Oh.' So she hadn't misunderstood him. 'I see,' she said, even though she really didn't see. How could he want her to go with him when he was just so…? Well, so…*much*. Of everything. And she so wasn't.

'You'd be doing me a huge favour,' he added, clasping his hands together and resting his bare forearms on his thighs, drawing her attention to the way the strong muscles stretched the fabric of his suit trousers and how the fly settled over the bulge of his…

Look away from his crotch! Are you insane?

'I have to go to this damn thing,' he said. 'And I prefer not to go alone.'

She stared at his face, hoping her heart wasn't going to punch right through her ribcage. He was actually serious. He wanted to take her to the Lumière Ball.

A part of her knew she should say no for the

good of her health. How on earth was she supposed to survive an event like that on this man's arm when she found discussing a spreadsheet in front of him a major challenge to her lung function?

Good Lord, had Imelda been right all along? Had he hired her to hit on her?

But, just as the coronary-inducing thought occurred to her, she recalled something else Imelda had said during their first meeting about her brother's dating habits.

Since he became a billionaire, women tend to chase him instead of the other way around, and he hates that.

Her lungs began to function again as Conall's motives became clear. He wasn't *really* hitting on *her*. He just didn't want to go to the Lumière Ball alone, because then he'd be fair game. And he hated that. This wasn't a real date, it was just a stunt date—to keep other women at bay. After all, he had said she'd be doing him a favour. That was all this was.

You've got this! No need to go to pieces. You can do him a favour and do yourself a massive favour too.

Because going to an event like the Lumière Ball would be the ultimate busman's holiday—event-planning-wise.

'The ball is tomorrow night…'

He was still talking in that deep, husky Irish accent that seemed to brush over her skin like a caress. She tried to listen.

'If your work schedule is a problem, I can ensure you're back in London by—'

'I'd love to go with you,' she interrupted him. 'If you're sure,' she added, suddenly scared he might change his mind.

His eyebrows rose up his forehead, but then he smiled. It was the first truly spontaneous smile she'd ever seen on his face. It set alight the mischievous sparkle in his eyes, adding silver streaks to the true blue and turning that damn dimple into a lethal weapon.

She couldn't breathe again, of course. But now she didn't care. The excitement flowed through her like an electrical current. Maybe this was a stunt date for him. But she intended to make the most of it. Why not? It had been so long since she'd been the focus of any man's attention.

Somehow Tom's attention had been different. Not electrifying but cosy,√ comfortable and kind.

She felt the inevitable wave of melancholy. But she could almost hear him talking to her again, the way he had on their wedding night, as they'd lain together on his hospital bed and listened to the monitor beeping.

'No guilt or sadness after this is over, Katie. And no sack cloth and ashes either, you promise? You

deserve to find someone else who can give you all the things I can't. Adventure, travel, a grand passion, lots and lots of kids... And really spectacular sex.'

She hadn't kept that promise, of course. Not for five years. Because she'd been gutted after losing Tom—and far too busy once she'd started her business—even to *want* to look for any of that stuff.

Plus, she was not daft enough to look for grand passion or great sex with a man like Conall O'Riordan. Because he was so far out of her league, it was ridiculous. And way too overwhelming. Making love for the first time with a man like him—who probably knew all the moves and could give a woman a multiple orgasm from thirty paces—would be dangerous. Because she was just vulnerable and chronically inexperienced enough to read far too much into it.

But adventure. And travel. And maybe even a little stunt passion. For one glorious heart-stopping weekend in Paris? That she could totally do.

'Grand,' Conall said. Then touched a thumb to her cheek. He slid it down to her chin to capture her face and lift it to his. For one glorious moment, anticipation squeezed her rib cage. Her heart stopped beating then started again at warp speed and her lips parted of their own accord. His gaze narrowed, the pupils dilating as her tongue darted out to wet suddenly arid lips. But, after staring at her mouth for what felt like a millennium or two, he cleared his throat, blinked and then dropped his hand.

And her heart dropped into her stomach, the intense yearning followed by devastation.

Yup, she definitely could not risk real passion with this man, or she would be risking so much more.

'How long will it take you to pack?' he asked.

It took her several moments to process the question—after her ludicrous overreaction to that almost-kiss.

'Not long,' she said. 'I don't have too much with me.'

'Grand,' he said again, then stood up and strode back around his desk to press the button on the intercom. 'Liam, get the chopper ready to take us to Knock, and then make sure Joe is available to fly us to Paris. Then call Etienne at the Hotel de la Lumière and extend my booking for the suites on the top floor to include tonight.'

'Yes, Con. What time do you want to leave?' came the prompt reply from his assistant through the speaker phone.

Con glanced at his watch. 'In about forty-five minutes.'

Katie stood slowly, feeling dazed now as well

as giddy. They were leaving *tonight*? In less than an hour?

Conall's gaze connected with hers as he signed off, and he let out a rough chuckle that sounded a little strained. 'You should probably get out of here and start packing, Cinderella.'

'Right, absolutely. On it.' She nodded and flew out of the office.

But it wasn't until she was in her suite, busy throwing things into her suitcase like a crazy person, while simultaneously tapping out a text to Caroline, her PA at Hamilton Events, to rearrange her schedule for Monday and trying not to hyperventilate, that it occurred to her Cinderella had a problem.

Not only did she not have anything remotely appropriate to wear to something as exclusive as the Lumière Ball in her luggage… She didn't have any spare *haute couture* lying around at home either.

And no fairy godmother to speak of.

Terrific. Cinderella has a ball-gown emergency.

CHAPTER SIX

'IT'S ALL SO much more magnificent than I ever imagined. And I imagined a lot.'

Katherine Hamilton's whisper was hoarse with awe, her head swivelling backwards and forwards to get the best possible angle to view the Arc de Triomphe as Conall drove across the intersection at L'Etoile.

'As you imagined?' Conall asked, far too aware of his passenger's scent, which had been torturing him for the last few hours and was now filling up the car's interior. 'Haven't you ever been to Paris?'

Surely that couldn't be true? Was that why she'd been so quiet on the flight over?

He'd wanted to quiz her about so many things. But he'd decided against it, until he could figure out how best to approach this situation. The decision to bring her to Paris had been done on the spur of the moment. A knee-jerk reaction to the desire that had been flooding his system for days now, and which he had finally acknowledged.

Why not admit it? The urge to bring Katherine to Paris had a lot less to do with getting the information he wanted about her brother than it did with the spike of need and determination that had assailed him the minute she'd said yes.

She'd looked so excited, so eager… And so nervous when she'd joined him in the chopper for their flight to Knock and then onward to Paris in the company jet. And somehow so young.

She had also seemed oddly overwhelmed by the luxury, which made no sense at all. Surely the lifestyle he had now wasn't that far removed from the one in which she'd been brought up? Surely it was a lifestyle she would be very familiar with, given the kind of clients she worked for? Event planners needed to look confident in this environment, and she had up till now. But, as they'd flown over the Irish Sea and English Channel and finally arrived at Orly an hour ago, she had seemed utterly captivated by the whole experience.

Was this another act—the awestruck ingénue? He was trying to convince himself it was. But something about the glow of enchantment in her gaze and the flush of excitement on her cheeks seemed entirely genuine. And it was starting to bother him.

Seducing her in his office at Kildaragh had seemed like a good idea three hours ago. Sex, after all, was nothing more than a biological urge. One they both appeared to have for each other. But now he was beginning to second-guess the impulse. Exactly how innocent was she? He knew from the detective's report she was twenty-four—very young to have founded her own event-planning business and made such a success of it. He had simply assumed she was worldly, given her work, her background and her business.

But now, seeing the wonder on her face, he was concerned he might have miscalculated. What if she wasn't as worldly as he had assumed? He'd already begun to suspect that, while she was incredibly good at what she did, she wasn't as hard-nosed as she should be.

But innocence would be far worse. Unlike her brother, he wasn't interested in seducing women with no experience. Women like his sister had been, who were vulnerable and naïve.

What was it about her that made him feel protective of her? Made him want to enhance this experience for her? He wasn't supposed to be that invested. It wasn't something he'd felt before for any woman—except maybe his sisters—and what he felt for Katherine certainly was not fraternal.

'Oh, no,' she said, that easy, even slightly shy smile spreading across her features and captivating him even more as she finally settled in her seat. 'Tom and I always talked about travelling, and we had Paris at the top of our list…' The glow on her cheeks dimmed. 'But we never got the chance.'

Who the hell is Tom?

Something that felt far too much like jealousy made Conall's hand jerk on the car's gear stick, the wistful tone telling him that, whoever this Tom guy was, he meant a great deal to Katherine.

The engine grunted in protest as he shifted back into gear to accelerate round a large delivery truck as they drove down the Champs-élysées.

'Who's Tom?' he found himself asking. Then wished he could take the question back. Tom, whoever he was, was clearly out of the picture now. Surely that was all that mattered?

She sighed, her eyes glittering as they headed down Paris's famous boulevard of lights—at a snail's pace, because it was choked with traffic. As always the bustle of movement and energy on the wide tree-lined avenue was intense. People filled the pavements, milling in and out of the street's grand terraces that housed cafés, theatres, cinemas and designer shops all buzzing with activity as night fell. Scooters zipped in and out of the traffic, irate drivers honked their horns and gesticulated and intrepid pedestrians stepped into the fray with typical Parisian *savoir faire.*

In the car, the mood had stilled, though becoming thick with an intimacy Conall had never intended but was somehow powerless to stop. He couldn't take the question back because he wanted to know the answer.

She glanced at him, the soft smile on her face both sad but so unguarded and full of compassion, it made him tense…and the jolt of envy increase. What was that about? Why should he care that no woman had ever looked at him like that, when he certainly did not want them to?

'Tom's my husband,' she said, so quietly he almost didn't hear her.

What the...? She was married. His fingers fisted on the steering wheel, but before he could even process his reaction to the shocking revelation she added, 'Or rather he was my husband. He died, five years ago. Not long after we were married. He was…'

She cleared her throat and he could hear the strain in her voice when she continued. 'He'd been sick for a long time.' She let out a rough laugh that sounded impossibly brave. 'But it's weird. I still can't think of him in the past tense.'

'You got married and widowed at nineteen?' he asked, unable to keep the incredulity out of his voice, and still not able to get his head round the furious envy caused by this insight into her past.

Why should he care about the man she'd married? Especially as the guy had died years ago. He already knew the woman was a romantic—she'd said so herself. Surely this just confirmed it?

But why did what she had done seem moving instead of desperately misguided? After all, if one of his own sisters had decided to marry some guy at that age, he would have advised against it. He didn't believe in love, and he believed even less in throwing your life away on a romantic idyll that could only bring you pain.

'You sound like you disapprove,' she said, her voice so devoid of judgement, he found himself defending his position, even though he knew her ill-advised marriage was none of his business.

'I do disapprove.'

'Why?' she asked. 'If I loved Tom, and he loved me, why wouldn't I marry him?'

He glanced at her. 'Do you really want me to answer that question?' he asked, knowing he probably shouldn't give her his opinion. After all, this wasn't meant to be more than a casual affair. Did he have the right to question her choices, however foolish?

But something about the way she'd phrased the question, as if she really couldn't figure out why marrying this guy had been a bad idea, got to him.

Seriously, there was romanticism and then there was self-destructiveness. And making a decision to hitch yourself to someone at that age, especially someone with no future, seemed naive in the extreme. It was pretty clear she was still hung up on this guy. Probably still thought she was in love with him. And that was mad, for all sorts of reasons.

'Yes, I really do,' she said.

'Then I'll tell you why.' He bit out the words, suddenly furious, the hole in his own chest that had been there for so many years making his tone sharper than he had intended. 'Because if your man Tom had ever really loved you, he would never have asked you to marry him in the first place.'

'Why not?' she asked, as if she really didn't get it.

'Because he knew he was going to leave you. That's a pretty crummy thing to do to someone you love. Don't you think?'

'You can't blame someone for dying, Mr O'Riordan,' she said with such dignity he felt a strange yank in his chest. He denied it, though. What the hell foolishness was this?

'Call me Conall, Katherine,' he said. 'And, yes, you can,' he added, suddenly angry with the man she'd married for putting the sheen of sadness in her soft green eyes. Which reminded him far too much of his sisters' faces as they stood over their mother's grave.

'Tom didn't have a choice,' she whispered.

'He had a choice about whether to take advantage of you, though, didn't he?' He could just imagine her—a young woman barely more than a girl, compassionate and easily led, just like his sister Carmel when she'd had the misfortune to encounter Ross De Courtney's charms.

'He didn't take advantage of me! We were best friends and I was the one who suggested marriage.'

'Why, though? So you could watch him die?'

'No, so I could watch him live what little life he had left.'

Good Lord, was she really that soft-hearted and that soft-headed? The man had exploited her. Used her. He said he'd loved her, but he'd hurt her. Wasn't that always the way when someone said they loved you?

She shifted round in her seat as the car cruised past the Jardin des Tuileries, the panoramic park crowded now with evening joggers, parents herding hyperactive children home and couples strolling arm-in-arm in the twilight.

'It's so beautiful,' she all but purred. 'And so

romantic,' she added, their conversation about her marriage clearly over.

He sealed up the anger in his heart and the painful memories. She was right. Giving her his opinion of her marriage wasn't what he had planned this evening.

She continued to remark on the sights—carried out of her sadness by the splendour of the City of Lights—and determined not to talk about her marriage any longer.

He'd always enjoyed Paris himself—perhaps because its cosmopolitan energy and sophistication were the antithesis of where he'd grown up in rural Ireland. But hearing the enthusiasm in her voice, seeing the excitement light up her face, had him seeing it in a new light.

'The French are so wonderfully sophisticated, aren't they?' she remarked. 'So steeped in culture, and yet so at ease with it. I love that about them.'

She turned back to him, her face flushed but her expression clearly keen to paper over the cracks their conversation had caused. 'I went on a skiing holiday once to the French Alps as a teenager. But I couldn't ski like the other pupils, so the teachers let me hang out at the resort while they took to the slopes. I adored it—going to the little *boulangerie* in the town square, trying out my faltering French on the shop keepers, checking out the local market.'

Something about her reaction—so genuine and fascinated—made the pulse of yearning in his chest intensify.

Don't be daft, Con.

Perhaps she'd never been to Paris before, but she had lived a privileged life. His sisters had certainly never been on a skiing holiday as teenagers. And neither had he.

'Why didn't you learn to ski as a child?' he asked, finally getting it together to press her for more information. 'If all your peers did?'

She laughed, the sound light, musical and self-deprecating. 'Mum didn't have money for skiing holidays. We basically lived from commission to commission—she was a talented artist, but she didn't believe in commercialising her work. And, anyway, I'm not exactly the sporty type.'

But your father was a millionaire...

He had to bite back the question before he gave away the fact he knew more about her background than he should. But even so the question tormented him. He knew Aldous De Courtney hadn't publicly acknowledged her when he'd been alive, but he'd assumed the bastard would have paid some kind of maintenance. Was abandoning their children a trait of the De Courtney men, then? Because it was beginning to appear so.

'If your mother didn't have money for skiing

holidays, how did you end up on that one?' he asked, risking a glance at her face as the traffic ground to a halt again.

The smile became wistful, the delight in her expression faltering. 'She died when I was fourteen and my brother became my guardian. My half-brother,' she clarified. 'Luckily for me, he was loaded.'

The tone suggested she was joking, but her voice caught. And he could hear the grief that still lingered for the woman who had died when Katherine had still been a girl.

'That's tough,' he said.

'What is?'

'To lose your mother so young,' he murmured. 'The same thing happened to my sisters and it was very hard on them.'

He'd known about the basic facts of her life from the detective report—all except her marriage—but somehow he hadn't really made the connection, until now, that she had suffered the same loss as his sisters. Why hadn't he? And why did it make him feel even more protective towards her?

It was stupid, just an unfortunate coincidence.

'And you,' she said, so softly he almost didn't hear her over the din from the traffic outside the car. 'It must have been very hard on you too.'

'I was eighteen when my mother died,' he said,

trying to quell the emotion in his chest. He didn't require her sympathy…or her compassion. He didn't even deserve it. And he certainly hadn't brought Katherine Hamilton to Paris to have a heart-to-heart with her about his childhood. Or to open up old wounds he had sealed up a long time ago.

He'd paid his dues to his sisters as best he could. Had worked hard and sacrificed to give them everything he was capable of. Maybe money and security would never compensate them for the loss of their mother, but there was nothing more he could do, so there was no point beating himself up about it. Especially in front of her.

'I was a grown man. It didn't affect me as badly.'

'Were you really a grown man at eighteen?' she asked.

He turned to find her watching him, her eyes so full of understanding, he flinched.

What the...?

'I earned my first million by the time I was twenty-one,' he said flatly, determined to take that soft glow from her face. 'I am driven, ambitious and ruthless when I need to be. But, most of all, I stopped being a boy long before my mother died.'

He dragged his gaze away, aware that he was

saying too much, that he was overreacting, but somehow unable to stop himself.

He crossed the Place de la Concorde and drove onto the forecourt of the Hotel de la Lumière. He braked the powerful BMW in front of the magnificent four-storey building that took up a whole city block—originally a neo-classical palace built for Louis XV, the landmark hotel's arches and columns had been designated an historic monument by the French government over a century ago.

O'Riordan Enterprises had booked out the whole top floor of the landmark hotel for the Lumière Ball.

This was the man he was now—able to afford the trappings of royalty. A luxury he had worked so hard to earn, always aware of how far he'd come from that ambitious farm boy who had wanted so much more for himself than four a.m. wake-up calls, mucking out stalls or herding cows into the milking shed before he'd even had breakfast. The boy who had fallen asleep over his school books each evening, which he usually had to read by the fire because the farm's ageing generator had cut out again…

He'd done what he'd needed to do to get away from the path his birthright had set him on. A path every O'Riordan had followed until now.

He wasn't ashamed of that. And he refused

to apologise for his ambition or his success. But Katherine Hamilton needed to know that, while he might be prepared to wine and dine her this weekend, to seduce her with a little of the romance she obviously craved—to get everything out of her he desired—he was no hero. And no grief-stricken child either. Nor had he ever been.

She had stopped gazing about, all her attention on him now. It made him uneasy, unsettled, and yet also strangely energised. No woman had ever been foolish enough to romanticise him before—not even Christy, who had wanted to marry him—but then Katherine didn't know him. Perhaps he should give her a taste of what she was getting herself into.

'I don't believe you,' she said.

The comment was audacious. And personal. Both delusional and yet also forthright.

He laughed, but the sound had no humour. The arousal darkening her irises made the yearning in his gut twist and tighten.

'You can believe what you want,' he said. He touched her cheek with his thumb, slid it down to glide across her lips.

She gasped, her irises dilating to black. The need in her gaze was as vicious as the tangle of desire in his gut.

Gripping her chin, he pulled her closer.

To hell with it. He'd been waiting to taste her

for hours now, ever since she'd agreed to go with him and he'd seen the yearning in her eyes. Hell, even before that. Ever since he'd raised his head that first day to find her watching him in his office, when he should have been focussed on finding out more about her brother, and instead all he'd wanted was to find out more about her.

He dipped his head, giving her time to object, but all he could hear was the staggered pant of her breathing, encouraging him. He settled his lips over hers.

She opened for him instinctively, the sob of excitement firing his senses as he ran his tongue across the cupid's bow that had tormented him all evening and tasted her.

He delved deep, controlling the kiss, satisfaction turning to desperation as her palms flattened against his abdomen and her fingers gripped his shirt, drawing him closer.

He cradled her neck and angled her face, desperate to take everything she had to give him.

The kiss became more, so much more than he could ever have imagined. The fire in his gut turned from a slow burn to a raging inferno. He explored the recesses of her mouth, sipped at her lips, tangled his tongue with hers. She shuddered, moaned, the sound both desperate and excited and...*shocked.*

He drew back sharply.

Her eyes were glassy, dazed, stunned—more awestruck than when she'd seen the Arc de Triomphe for the first time—but then she blinked and jerked away.

'You… You kissed me?' she said.

He frowned, forced himself to drop his hand and deny the urge to grip her waist and drag her across the console into his lap, to press the hard weight of his erection into the hot cradle of her sex.

He could smell her arousal, which was even more addictive than the intoxicating scent of orange, rosemary and the taste of her lips.

But the shock was there, too.

He'd turned into an animal. The sophistication he'd worked so hard to attain over the last thirteen years—ever since the boy had made a vow to become a man—had deserted him as soon as his lips touched hers.

'Of course I did,' he said, realising he'd said it more sharply than he'd intended when he saw her blink. 'I've been wanting to for hours.'

She touched her finger to her lips, sill dazed, drawing his gaze to where he'd reddened the skin on her chin and cheek. He'd mauled her like a needy boy, instead of the man he knew himself to be.

What the heck was wrong with him?

'But I thought… I thought this was a stunt date?' she said.

'A what?' he asked, confused now as well as frustrated, with himself as much as her. When had he become a slave to his own appetites, unable to control his desires?

As much of a bastard as her brother.

'A stunt date…' she repeated, still making no sense whatsoever. 'I thought you asked me to the ball so you wouldn't have to fend off advances from other women. Your sister said you don't like to be chased. She said—'

'Imelda was wrong,' he cut in. Trust Imelda to have something to do with the shocked look in Katherine's eyes. 'This isn't a "stunt date", Katherine,' he added, drawing on the last reserves of his patience, still not sure how everything had got out of control so quickly and so comprehensively. 'I want you, and I believe you want me,' he continued, determined to be open with her. Or as open as he could be in the circumstances. 'And I'd say that kiss confirms it.'

He waited for her to deny it.

'I… Yes, I suppose it does.'

He noticed the parking valet standing patiently beside the car, waiting for them to get out. The boy seemed flushed.

He'd probably seen that kiss.

Conall might have been annoyed—he didn't

usually maul women with an audience—but the craven hunger still pounding in his groin was making it hard for him to think about anything but finishing what they'd started.

'I'm not in the business of pressuring women,' he said. 'If you want to go back to London, now you know this is not a stunt date, it can be arranged.'

He'd never considered himself to be a particularly gallant man, but something about the way she had kissed him…her response so fresh, so eager, so unguarded…had shocked him a little…and only made him more hungry. But still he waited patiently for her answer, or as patiently as he could with the need throbbing like a sore tooth.

At last, she shook her head. 'I don't want to go home.'

'Good.' He signalled the young man and concentrated on getting out of the car before he took what he wanted too soon. She needed time to adjust to the inevitable, and clearly so did he. When they made love, he intended to be in control.

'Bonsoir, mademoiselle,' the boy said to Katherine as he opened the car's passenger door.

Conall stepped out the other side, only too aware that he was still sporting a fairly impressive erection. A blast of the cold night air helped it to subside as two doormen took their luggage and the parking valet got into the car to drive it away.

He directed Katherine into the marble and gilt-edged lobby, the antique furniture in keeping with the hotel's historic grandeur. But, as he placed his palm on the small of her back, he became far too aware of her shudder. And had to steel himself against the desire to move his hand lower and cup the lush weight of her backside in the form-fitting coat.

They were whisked to the front of the queue to check in and then directed to the top floor. He walked her to her suite, keeping his hands to himself.

Gone were her gasps of astonishment, the babbling commentary on everything she saw. Instead she was quiet, subdued, contemplative. But he could still sense the ripple of reaction as they stopped at the door to her rooms.

He turned her towards him, touched his thumb to her lip and then brushed it tenderly over the skin of her chin.

'I should have shaved. Your skin is very sensitive,' he said, rather inanely. It was about as close as he could get to an apology for taking her mouth in the car like a madman.

She nodded, watching him with those wide, transparent eyes again.

'Liam suggested you might need a stylist,' he

managed, remembering the enquiry he'd had from his assistant, suddenly not wanting to let her go. Knowing it was going to be a very long while before he could get to sleep after that kiss. 'To get you something to wear for the ball,' he prompted. 'He figured you might not have anything appropriate.'

He could have asked one of his assistants to deal with this tomorrow. He'd always intended to when Liam had mentioned the problem. But, when the blush lit the sprinkle of freckles on her nose, he was glad he hadn't.

'Actually, that would be great. I need to buy something to wear. But I have no idea where to go in Paris.'

No way are you buying your own ball gown, he thought, but didn't say. Women's fashions were hardly his forte, but he suspected a suitable gown would be well outside her budget, and he'd be damned if he'd feel guilty about that too.

'Liam can handle it,' he said, still not quite able to draw his finger away from her flushed flesh.

What else was there to say? The kiss had been phenomenal. Much more than he had expected. But he needed to get this yearning under control before he saw her again. 'I'm going to be busy tomorrow, in meetings, so I'll be here at eight to take you down to the ball.'

'Okay,' she said.

Leaning forward, feeling her heartbeat pummelling against his thumb, he pressed a chaste kiss to her forehead then let her go. 'Enjoy yourself tomorrow.'

So saying, he turned and strode away.

Somehow, between now and eight tomorrow night, he needed to get a grip on this hunger. Or they were never going to make it to the damn ball.

Katie closed the door, caught the breath she had been holding and sunk down onto her bum, her back dragging against the door as her knees turned to water.

The city lights glittered through the huge arched windows that looked out onto a stone terrace. Moonlight lit up the palatial living area, glowing over bespoke antique furniture, luxury fabrics and expertly displayed art.

She drew in a staggered breath, catching the whiff of lemon polish, to inflate lungs constricted with shock and awe… The view of Paris from the penthouse suite was almost as breathtaking as Conall's kiss.

Almost.

She touched one trembling finger to her chin, smarting from the sting of beard scruff. Then ran it across her mouth, her lips burning from the ferocity of his kiss.

Almost? Who was she kidding?

The view of Paris—a city she'd wanted to visit for years—was nowhere near as spectacular as Conall O'Riordan's kiss.

He'd devoured her, as if he couldn't get enough of her, his lips hungry, seeking, branding her and demanding her surrender. And it had lit a fire inside her body which she hadn't even realised was there. And had made it burn.

She crossed her legs and sat dumbly, trying to get her breathing to even out, aware of everywhere her body buzzed, pulsed and throbbed.

She should get up, switch on the light, explore the suite—which was probably as magnificent as everything else about this trip—and check out the no doubt heart-stopping view from the terrace.

But she couldn't move. Her body was like warm butter—melted, insubstantial, a puddle of sensation.

What had happened? One minute he'd been chastising her about Tom and her marriage—reminding her far too forcefully of her brother—and the next… She sighed, the guilty flush working its way up her neck.

'Oh, Tom, I'm sorry,' she whispered into the darkness. But Tom's face seemed so hazy now.

Tom had never made her feel the way Conall O'Riordan just had. He'd always been a boy, never able to grow to manhood. He'd been her best friend. But had he ever really been her husband? she wondered. In any meaningful sense…?

The trickle of guilt became a flood. Not because she'd responded so readily to Conall's kiss—his scent, his texture, his taste, all so addictive—but because she couldn't even really remember any more what it had been like to kiss Tom.

She'd loved him so much. But she was beginning to wonder if she had ever really *loved* him. Like an adult. Their life together felt like a dream now—a short, tragic, far away dream—with no conflict, no disagreements but also in some ways no substance, no excitement.

Why had she really married him? Had it been because he needed her, or because she'd needed him?

She cut off the thought. Her life with Tom was over, but one thing was for certain—that part of her life had not prepared her to deal with kissing a man like Conall O'Riordan.

And not stunt kissing either. *Real* kissing.

She took a few moments more to get her bearings back—which took a while, as her mind kept reliving that kiss—but after about five minutes she finally managed to drag her aching body off the floor.

She still felt shaky as she made her way

through the huge room to the terrace. Sliding open the glass doors, she found herself on a large stone balcony furnished with elegant loungers and huge flower arrangements made up of winter blooms and pine branches. But it was the view that took her breath away…

The Eiffel Tower stood like a beacon in the distance, the nearby glass and wrought-iron dome of the Grand Palais also lit up in the night.

Paris was a staggeringly beautiful city. And she was here for the first time. With a man who quite literally took her breath away. And he wanted her. *Really* wanted her, with the same urgency she wanted him.

She should be cautious and careful. She still wasn't sure the ethics of what she was doing were exactly right. Was he her boss? Would she jeopardise the commission if she took what he was offering this weekend?

She had to hope not. She knew she was doing a good job with the wedding planning, and he'd seemed a lot less interested in any of it once Imelda had taken over.

She had to believe whatever happened in Paris would stay in Paris. He'd said as much. She certainly knew he wasn't a man who did long term.

Her heart slowed as she recalled the frustrated expression on his face when they'd talked about her marriage. It had been so weird. Perhaps she should have taken offence…his objections to it were not unlike her brother's…but somehow she'd had the strangest feeling they weren't really talking about her choices, her past, but his…

He'd been determined to convince her he was ruthless, unfeeling, unemotional. That his interest in her past had been pure curiosity or arrogance. But it had felt like more than that, especially when he'd spoken about being a man at eighteen.

Maybe he believed that. But she wasn't convinced.

She shut off the direction of her thoughts.

Stop over-thinking this weekend when you're already in danger of being swept off your feet.

She wanted to enjoy herself. To go to her first ever ball. To finally find out what all the fuss about sex was, something Conall O'Riordan could surely show her.

But she had to remember this was a fleeting moment, a glorious adventure, nothing else.

It didn't mean anything more than some spectacular chemistry and a hunger which she would finally have a chance to feed.

She took a deep breath and let it out slowly, her gaze taking in the spectacular view, her body remembering another view even more spectacular: Conall's deep-blue gaze fixed on her face before he'd branded her with his kiss.

You deserve this chance...these two days out of real life.

A smile snuck onto her lips, making her even more aware of the burn from Conall's ferocious kiss.

Cinderella, eat your heart out! Katie Hamilton is going to the ball.

CHAPTER SEVEN

'THIS COLOUR LOOKS incredible on you! The jewelled bodice is perfect to bring out the emerald in your eyes, *mademoiselle*.'

The stylist, Celestine Dupre, purred next to Katie's shoulder as Katie gazed at herself in the gilt-edged full-length mirror in Madame Laurent's luxury boutique in the Marais. Her fingertips touched the beading on the gown's bodice, then traced the neck line that dipped to reveal the swell of her cleavage.

A blush mottled the skin. Thank goodness for the bustier Celestine had insisted she put on, or she'd be spilling out of the gown all together.

She swished her hips from side to side and watched the gown's hem glide over the jewelled slippers which Celestine had insisted she wear with the outfit.

Katie let out a shuddery breath. She wanted this gown. It gave her confidence and made her feel...*special*. 'How much is it?'

She forced herself to downgrade her excitement. The designer creation was exquisite, the beaded emerald satin fitted to make her curves look like a work of art. She'd never felt more like a princess in her entire life. But the stylist Conall had hired, and Madame Laurent, the boutique's French couturier, and her staff had been super-cagey about the cost of every gown she'd tried on so far.

She ran a successful company. She wasn't a pauper, but paying thousands for a gown she would probably only get to wear once was not a good use of her resources.

Celestine sent her a benevolent smile. 'Monsieur O'Riordan's assistant said you are not to worry about the price, that Monsieur O'Riordan is paying for…'

'She'll take it.'

Katie gasped and swung round at the assertive statement, delivered in a far too familiar Irish accent, as goose bumps rioted over her skin.

Conall strode towards her. He looked tall and indomitable in black jeans, a dark polo-neck sweater and a leather jacket—a stark and defiantly masculine presence in the boudoir's elegant cream and satin interior.

'Conall?' she murmured, the goose bumps going haywire as his penetrating gaze raked over her, and she suddenly became far too aware of all the places where the gown clung. And every inch of skin it exposed, which was rather a lot.

'It looks perfect for tonight, and it suits you,' he said, taking her fingers and lifting her arm away from her body so he could get a better look.

'Why…? Why are you here?' she asked, feeling stupidly shy and yet also ridiculously happy to see him. Whatever the gown cost, she would find a way to pay for it. She wanted him to look at her like this all night.

'The meetings finished early,' he said, his assessing gaze finally rising back to her face. 'I thought I could give you a tour of Paris. As you've never been to the city before.'

'Really? That would be amazing,' she said, her heart lifting into her throat and battering her collar bone.

Today already felt like a fairy tale. She'd been introduced to Celestine by Conall's assistant Liam, and the stylist had whisked her off to a luxury spa straight after breakfast where she had been buffed, primped and polished to within an inch of her life by a team of beauticians and hair stylists. Then Celestine had taken her to the Marais in a limousine and introduced her to one of France's most famous *modistes*. They'd been working out an outfit for the ball ever since, beginning with shoes and underwear and finally moving on to the perfect gown.

She'd always been a bit of a tomboy when it came to clothes. But she knew amazing craftsmanship when she saw it.

She turned to the couturier, whom she knew didn't speak English. *'D'accord, madame. Je voudrais l'acheter,'* she said in her faltering French, hoping the woman understood. Then she spoke to Celestine. 'Could you ask her to send the bill to the Hotel de la Lumière?'

Celestine nodded but, instead of translating the information, her gaze moved to Conall. 'Monsieur O'Riordan?'

Conall rattled something off in fluent French to Celestine and then the couturier. The older woman beamed, nodding and smiling, and then clicked her fingers to have her assistants help Katie out of the gown.

But before Katie was led away she turned back to Conall. 'What did you just say to her?'

'I have an account here, Katherine,' he said. 'The gown is on me.'

'But I can't let you pay for it…' she began, shocked at the thrill that worked its way up her spine at the thought that he would even offer.

What was wrong with her? She was an independent woman. Conall wasn't her boyfriend, not really, and she certainly did not need him to buy her clothes.

'Consider it a business expense,' he said,

riding roughshod over her objection as he spoke again in French to the couturier and her assistants.

'But it's not…' she said. She didn't even know how much it cost yet, but it had to be in the thousands, and how was he going to justify that as a business expense?

Then something else he had said occurred to her. 'Why do you have an account at a ladies' couturier…?'

His lips twisted in a mocking grin that made him look even more devastating than usual and he dropped his voice, leant close and murmured in her ear. 'Why do you think, Katherine? FYI, I don't wear a lot of designer gowns myself.'

She choked out a laugh. But the blush already glowing on her collar bone blazed its way up her neck, making her feel like the most gauche woman on the planet.

Of course he had an account at one of Paris's most exclusive boutiques. Because she wasn't the first woman he'd invited here and she wouldn't be the last.

'I'd… I'd still prefer to pay for my own ball gown,' she managed.

The smile became rueful. But then he spoke again to the couturier and got a reply. Turning back, he said, 'It costs a hundred and fifty thousand euros.'

'It... *What?*' Her jaw almost dislocated, it dropped so fast. Her stunned gaze dipped to stare at the exquisite gown. At the intricate stitching, the jewels glowing in the sparkle of afternoon sunlight.

Good grief, are they real emeralds?

'I... I should find something less expensive,' she managed. Her company made a decent profit but a hundred and fifty thousand euros for one dress? She couldn't possibly justify that kind of expenditure.

'No need,' he said, still grinning and making her feel even more ridiculous. She worked on luxury event-planning, so she knew a little bit about how these people lived. Why on earth hadn't she figured out the price would be much more than she could afford?

'We really don't have time for you to look for another one if we want to see any of the sights this afternoon. And why should we, when this one is grand?' he said, stepping back and treating her to another oxygen-depriving assessment. 'I've got this.'

Before she had a chance to argue further, he placed warm, callused palms on her bare shoulders, turned her round so that she was facing the changing area and then gave her a soft pat on her bottom. 'Now, go get changed, so we can get the hell out of here. There's so much I want to show you and we only have four hours before the ball.'

The giddy thrill that blossomed under her breastbone at his playful tone propelled her towards the changing room before she had a chance to argue.

Perhaps she could work out a payment plan, she thought frantically as the assistants helped her out of the gown, and she watched them box up the exquisite dress while she tugged on her jeans, boots and jacket.

She really couldn't accept a one-hundred-and-fifty-thousand-euro gift, but she could always arrange to return the gown once she'd worn it, or auction it online and recoup some of the cost to pay Conall back that way.

The giddy thrill worked its way into her stomach. She'd figure it out somehow. One thing she refused to do was let a little thing like an astronomically expensive ball gown get in the way of their afternoon adventure.

She couldn't wait to see Paris with Conall O'Riordan and take the opportunity to get to know him better. She already planned to sleep with him tonight but, given that he was going to be her first lover, why shouldn't she want to know more about him?

Maybe this wasn't a proper relationship, but it was a proper date—leading in one very intimate direction later tonight. Surely she was entitled to satisfy some of her curiosity?

'But where's the car?' Katherine chewed on her bottom lip, sending the usual spike of adrenaline straight into Conall's gut. Not good when he had to negotiate Parisian traffic while she clung on to him for dear life.

Conall mounted the gleaming vintage Harley-Davidson he'd had delivered to the hotel an hour ago—as soon as he'd called off the rest of the day's meetings, knowing he had been struggling to focus all morning and was not going to be able to stay away from Katherine for another twenty-five minutes, let alone four hours.

Perhaps it was indulgent and reckless, but he'd been rewarded when he'd walked into the exclusive boutique, where his last two girlfriends had enjoyed shopping, and had seen the woman he was taking to the ball tonight in all her glory.

She'd looked stunning in the figure-hugging gown… He'd pay a million euros to escort her in that dress tonight, let alone one hundred and fifty thousand. And a million more to ease her out of it later.

He cut off the rampant direction of his thoughts with an effort.

Not the time.

First, he had to give her the tour of Paris he'd

offered her. Why hadn't he just suggested going back to the hotel? But something had stopped him. Even though he knew, from last night's kiss and the flushed determination on her face after it, she was more than willing…

Something he wasn't quite sure of. Maybe it was the surprising way she'd reacted to his perfectly reasonable decision to pay for the gown. Or the way she was now chewing her delectable bottom lip, as she stared at the bike as if he were asking her to ride a fire-breathing dragon.

'But I've never ridden on a motorbike before,' she murmured, raising her panicked gaze to his.

He had to choke back a laugh at her look of concern. 'It's perfectly safe. And the best way to see Paris when we're this close to rush hour.'

After straddling it, he adjusted the clutch, flicked up the stand and stamped down on the ignition peddle. The bike roared to life, making Katherine jump.

He grinned. He couldn't help it, this was going to be fun. And when was the last time he'd had fun with a woman, or anybody, for that matter? His life had been so damn serious and focussed for so long, but there was something about Katherine Hamilton—her eagerness, her earnestness, but also her determination and guts—that made him want to show her Paris his way. Because he knew she'd appreciate it.

He grabbed a helmet from the bike's saddle bag and lobbed it to her. She caught it instinctively. 'Put that on and climb aboard.'

'But...' She glanced down at the helmet. 'The stylist spent an hour this morning doing my hair for the ball,' she managed.

He studied her hair. The curls had been scrunched in some concoction and arranged to halo around her head in artful disarray. The do was great, drawing attention to her peach-soft skin, high cheekbones and those eyes—now wide with panic and astonishment, but also curiosity and excitement.

She wanted to do this. She just needed a bit of a nudge. Katherine had curtailed her adventurous spirit for years, the way he'd curtailed his own. He could feel it in his bones. Married at nineteen to a man who had died a few weeks later, struck down by grief and then focussed on making a success of her business. She hadn't had the time to indulge herself any more than he'd had after becoming guardian to his sisters at eighteen and working flat out to make his mark.

This afternoon was a chance for them both to throw off the chains of responsibility and cut loose for a few hours. And he wasn't going to let her chicken out.

'The hair can be fixed,' he said, knowing full well the hair wasn't really the issue. She hadn't struck him as a woman who was vain about her appearance. If she was, she would never have turned up for their meeting in Kildaragh in muddy jeans, and she would have known the cost of the gown—and been more than happy to have him foot the bill.

Her gaze met his, purpose igniting the gold streaks in her emerald eyes and banishing the last of her indecision.

Damn, but he loved how transparent she was. How easy she was to read. There seemed to be no subterfuge with this woman, no desire or inclination to hide her feelings or hold back. Why he should find that so captivating, he had no idea. But he chose not to question it too deeply. She was just refreshingly different from the women he usually dated, that was all. The novelty would wear off soon enough once they'd fed this insistent hunger. But why not enjoy the ride? He'd once loved the chase, after all, he just hadn't had the chance to indulge in it for a very long time.

She placed the helmet on her head, the determined expression almost as beautiful as the flush highlighting her cheeks. 'Okay, fine, let's do this thing.'

He laughed, the chuckle a little rusty but still making his ribs tighten. 'Grand. Climb aboard, Cinderella,' he said, getting into the spirit of the thing. 'Your steed awaits.'

ments. Or make too much of the sense of connection that had grown during the afternoon. But for once he looked completely open and unguarded.

'How do you know Paris so well?' she asked. 'Do you come here a lot?' she added, then felt her cheeks warm.

Fabulous, Katie, why not just ask him if he comes here often?

He simply stared at her for a moment, making her sure he was going to deflect the probing question, as he had the few times she'd already asked him about himself today. They'd shared a strong coffee on a barge on the Seine in the shadow of Notre Dame and toured the haunting statuary in the Père Lachaise Cemetery, where he pointed out the burial places of everyone from Jim Morrison to Abelard and Héloïse.

But anticipation rose like a bubble in her chest as he turned away from her to look out across the stunning vista. The smile had been replaced by a pensive look—was he finally going to answer a personal question?

When he spoke, his voice rough with memory, she found herself letting go of the breath she hadn't realised she was holding… Why did this feel so important?

'I lived here for a year, after I sold the farm in Galway. I'd set up Rio Corp two years before, and it was doing well. We had patents for a lot of really innovative agricultural equipment, but I wanted to learn French so we could base our European hub in Paris.' He let out a slow breath. 'My sisters weren't too happy about it. At that point they were fourteen and sixteen and they'd never left Ireland—learning French was not high on their list of priorities,' he finished, the wistful chuckle filled with affection.

'You brought your sisters with you?' she asked, stupidly touched. She'd always longed for a close-knit family who chose to stay together, no matter what. But still it surprised her to think he hadn't simply had his sisters carted off to boarding school while he'd taken his business to the next level. He had been a young man, still only twenty-three, already burdened with so much.

Conall's head swung towards her, his brows lifting. 'Of course. Why wouldn't I?' he asked, the simple question making the inadequacy she thought she'd conquered a lifetime ago squeeze her chest.

Why not, indeed?

While she'd yearned for her brother's attention in the early years after her mother's death, and had been unbearably lonely at the exclusive school he'd sent her to, she had always believed she'd understood why he'd had to send her away. But now she wasn't so sure. She could still remember those pitiful phone calls when she'd begged him to let her stay with him over the holidays, not to leave her at the school when all the other kids had gone home to their families, but his answer had always been the same.

'I'm not your father, Katie. And I'm not cut out to be a parent. Believe me, you're much better off where you are.'

Why had she never realised until this moment that the problem hadn't been with her, it had been with him? If Conall O'Riordan could be a parent to his sisters, why hadn't her brother been able to step up to the plate too, even if only for a few weeks over the holidays? She'd asked him for so little in the way of emotional support. But he'd given her even less.

'Well, I guess...' She stumbled as Conall's eyes narrowed on her face, almost as if he could see into her thoughts, her feelings. Instinctively she tried to mask the stab of inadequacy and hurt, that painful instinct that told her she was 'less than', that she was somehow unlovable.

Ross had been right about one thing: he had never been capable of being a brother to her in the truest sense of the word. How stupid of her not to realise that until this moment.

'It just seems you would have had a lot on your plate already,' she managed. 'Relocating to Paris with two teenage girls must have been tough. Especially if they weren't keen on the move.'

'You have no idea.' He let out a gruff laugh, but it was so full of affection, her heart squeezed again. What must it be like to have someone love you no matter what?

Even her mother had always set conditions on her affection—showing it only as long as Katie didn't get in the way when she was busy with a piece, didn't ask too much or make a fuss when they moved again on an artistic whim. She'd been uprooted so many times as a child, she had been forced to learn resilience and adaptability. She'd gained the ability to settle into new places with optimism and hope, always determined to see the best in any new spot.

But it had also left her yearning for stability. Maybe just not the stability of an exclusive boarding school where everyone judged you for your 'common' accent, your complete failure to conjugate a Latin verb correctly and the fact that your older brother, who paid the fees, didn't seem to be interested in spending any time with you.

'Imelda came around a lot quicker than Carmel,' Conall murmured, the warmth in his voice unguarded now. 'Immy could be a troublemaker, but it isn't in her nature to sulk. She's too much of a livewire. Mel, on the other hand, is a born rebel—super-smart, super-headstrong and super-independent. Boy, did she know how to crucify me for all the wrongs I was doing her by taking her away from her mates. She's nobody's pushover,' he continued. 'Or at least she didn't used to be,' he said, so softly she almost didn't catch the words.

'Mel is the one who has a son?' she asked, keen to keep him talking about his sisters, if for no other reason than it softened those gruff edges and gave her another precious insight into his family life.

His gaze locked on hers, the suspicious look startling her as the expression on his face hardened. Had she said something wrong?

'Yeah,' he said at last, the sharp tone unmistakeable. 'Some rich, entitled bastard seduced her when she was nineteen, a virgin, got her pregnant, then insisted Mac wasn't his son. It changed her. But she's so damn tough, she refused to take any help from me. She wouldn't even tell me who the guy was.'

She could hear the brittle fury in his tone. Whoever his nephew's father was, the man was probably very lucky Carmel had never told her brother his name, or she doubted he'd be able to father any more children.

'I'm so sorry. He sounds like a jerk,' she said.

'He is, but Carmel and Mac are better off without him, so there's that. And she's a terrific mammy,' he said, his admiration for his sister clear. 'Mac doesn't need that bastard in his life.'

'Especially as he has you,' she said, remembering what Imelda had said about how close Conall was to his nephew.

She stifled the silly sting of envy, for everything the O'Riordans had. How foolish, she thought, to be jealous of a little boy, especially one who had been rejected by his father. She knew what that felt like.

'Yeah, he has me,' Conall said. 'I'd never let anyone hurt him, certainly not that son of a...' He cut off the curse word, but his gaze remained locked on her face, and for one awful moment it seemed as if his anger was directed at her...

But then he broke eye contact and murmured, 'Sorry, it's a sore point.' The apology was grudging at best, but she took it at face value. Because if she had learned one thing about Conall O'Riordan in the last twenty-four hours it was that beneath the veneer of control was a man of fierce passions, especially where his family was concerned.

'I understand,' she said, because she really did. She placed her fingers on his arm, the jolt of awareness arrowing down when his forearm flexed. 'My father never acknowledged me,' she said gently.

Perhaps it was too much information. It was also something she never spoke about to anyone, but she became convinced it was the right thing to do when he looked at her again and the raw fury had dimmed.

'It hurt to know that he didn't ever want me. That he didn't ever value me. That I was a mistake. My mother always insisted it didn't matter, that it didn't make me "less than", but it felt like somehow it did. And when she died I was terrified I'd have to go into care. That I was totally alone. So when my brother Ross got in touch…'

She sighed. She could still remember that day—how she'd run up to this tall, handsome stranger and hugged him too tightly. And how he had stiffened but hadn't drawn back. Instead he had patted her shoulders awkwardly. He had tried to make things right, even though he'd had no idea how to deal with a grieving child.

Ross could have abandoned her—she had no doubt he had wanted to, but he hadn't—and for that she would always be grateful. He'd fed her, clothed her, paid for the most expensive schools and then college and, most importantly of all, he hadn't hesitated to acknowledge her as his half-sister. Ross had tried to be there for her in the only way he'd known how, even though it had clearly gone against every one of his instincts. Instincts she was sure had been drummed into him by a man who she was probably very lucky had never wanted to be her father after all.

'Well, it made a difference,' she said. 'We

haven't spoken in a long time… Ross was as opposed to my marriage to Tom as you were.' She huffed out a breath, determined to forgive her brother his failings. She was a grown woman now and she had survived. It was foolish to still need his approval.

'But he was there when I needed him the most.' She sent Conall what she hoped was an easy, well-adjusted smile—strangely gratified to see him watching her intently. 'A strong male role model is what children need. Ross wasn't up to the job of surrogate father, not really, but the fact he tried is what mattered. The thing is, Mac knows that you love him. So you're right—he doesn't need this man, if he has you.'

So that bastard abandoned her too.

Conall's heart pulsed hard as he tried to contain his violent reaction to her quiet revelation.

Her loyalty to a man who clearly didn't deserve it disturbed him in a way he wasn't sure how to handle. Because it only made him feel more protective towards her. And that couldn't be good.

Katherine is far too sweet and forgiving for her own good.

He touched her cheek, letting his thumb glide down the flushed skin—finally forced to let go the last of the resentment he'd wanted to feel towards her.

'Good to know,' he murmured, a little choked up by her faith in him, however misplaced.

He cleared his throat, let his hand drop. 'So, where do you want to go next?'

She smiled, the spontaneous grin as trusting as the rest of her. 'Where do you want to take me?'

Back to the hotel.

He stifled the thought and the shudder of need that went with it. What was it about her openness, and her honesty, that made her even more desirable to him?

That way lay danger, he realised. The feeling of connection, and the riot of emotions she caused, was not something he should take too lightly until he knew how to handle them.

'How about we get some food? I'm starving,' he said, even though he knew food wasn't going to vanquish the driving hunger in his gut. 'I know a grand little brasserie—looks like something out of a film—where they do the best *moules-frites* in town.'

'That sounds fabulous,' she said, her eyes sparking with delight again, her pure *joie de vivre* infectious. 'I certainly worked up an appetite with all those steps,' she added. But he could hear the heat in her voice, too, matching his own. And knew the meal was going to be pure torture.

'The Eiffel Tower was so much bigger than I expected,' Katie said breathlessly, unable to contain the burst of joy as Conall gripped her freezing fingers, his hand warm against hers, and steered her through the hotel lobby. Heads turned, probably because she was with the handsomest man in the whole of Europe… And perhaps also because they were trailing a puddle of water behind them on the marble tiles.

'I wish we had been able to go up it. I bet the view's phenomenal,' she added as he stabbed the call button for the penthouse lift.

'It is… But are you mad?' he added, but he was smiling, that rare smile she had become addicted to. 'We would have drowned.'

She laughed. She didn't know why she amused him so much—probably her total inability to be remotely sophisticated or blasé about all the amazing things he'd shown her today—but she was glad she did. Because she suspected that, despite all his wealth and success, and the strong, loving family he had spent his life nurturing, Conall O'Riordan didn't smile nearly often enough.

They'd wound their way across Paris on his

powerful bike after leaving Sacre Coeur, to a brasserie tucked away on a side street near the Place de la Bastille. It was all chrome fittings and leather booths separated by glass etched with drawings of elegant ladies straight out of a Toulouse-Lautrec painting. The smoke-stained walls and delicious plates of mussels and French fries had made her feel as though she'd stepped back to an elegant time of dancing girls and top-hatted gentlemen.

Back on the bike they'd wound their way through the cobble-stoned streets of the Marais, and the bustling markets of Les Halles. The Eiffel Tower had been their final stop but, just as Conall had been bribing the attendant—because apparently billionaires didn't queue—the heavens had opened. She'd been soaked through within minutes, clinging to Conall as they'd raced back to the hotel, all her senses focussed on the feel of his body—strong, solid, smelling of clean pine soap and motor oil and wet leather—and the pulsing ache between her thighs that had been building all afternoon.

Could any day have been more wonderful?

She hadn't managed to prise any more information out of him about his life, his past, himself. While he was fairly comfortable talking about his sisters, she had soon realised Conall was almost preternaturally close-lipped when it came to the subject of himself. But then he hadn't asked her for any more confidences either… So, after a few more faltering attempts that had been easily rebuffed, she'd resolved not to pry. If this fling was going to work, she needed to stow her curiosity about him and live in the present, live in the now. Enjoy what this weekend was—and not get hung up on what it wasn't.

Conall O'Riordan had given her Paris. But, so much more than that, he'd made her feel seen, feel special, feel like a woman—who was desired—for the first time in her life. She let the excitement swell in her chest and pound between her thighs as he dragged her into the lift.

He tugged her back until they were standing against the back wall of the ornate steel enclosure, then tipped up her chin and wiped the moisture from her cheeks with his thumbs.

She shuddered, the ripple of reaction shooting up her spine, as it had so many times during the afternoon, every time she'd felt his back shift against her breasts or his arm fall across her shoulders to tug her to his side when he was pointing out some interesting sight or other.

'You're freezing,' he murmured. 'And soaked.' He glanced at his watch. 'The ball begins in twenty minutes,' he said. 'How long do you need before I can come and get you? I have no problem being fashionably late.'

It took her a moment to register what he was saying, as her chest deflated like a popped party balloon.

But I don't want to go to the ball. I want to spend the rest of the night just with you.

The fanciful thought flashed into her head, the yearning so intense it took her a moment to process it. She blinked, struggling to get a grip on the desperate longing.

Don't be ridiculous.

They had come to Paris to attend the Lumière Ball together. It was one of the most prestigious events in Europe's social calendar. *Of course* she wanted to go to it, if for no other reason than it would be an incredible networking opportunity.

'Not long,' she managed at last, all her attempts to talk herself out of the reckless need doing nothing to silence the thrum of anticipation in her sex, or the hollow ache in her chest.

They had all night. There was no need to rush any of this. In fact, it might be better not to. Her emotions were already too close to the surface, her desire for this man well beyond the physical already.

He guided her down the corridor, stopping at the door to her suite. 'Good,' he said. 'I can't wait to see you in that dress…' His voice lowered to a husky purr as his gaze roamed over her, igniting all the spots that wanted to beg him to stay. 'And get you out of it again.'

The desire in her belly ignited at his parting comment.

Goodness, how am I going to survive the biggest social event of my life while imagining Conall O'Riordan seeing me naked?

CHAPTER NINE

THE LUMIÈRE BALL was everything it had been cracked up to be, and so much more.

Beautiful people graced the hotel's elegant parlours and ball rooms, dressed in the finest designer gowns and expertly tailored tuxedos. The huge glass atrium at the centre of the historic building had been turned into a lavish banqueting salon worthy of the stone palace's original owner, Louis XV.

The guests spilled out after a five-course *cordon bleu* supper into the main ball room, its vaulted ceiling lit by an array of antique chandeliers. Two wide, sweeping staircases—their stone balustrades entwined with glittering lights and winter blooms—led down from a first-floor balcony crowded with waiting staff in nineteenth-century livery, who served yet more glasses of vintage champagne in crystal flutes, delicate canapés for anyone still hungry and exotic cocktails in dazzling primary colours.

The whole experience was an event planner's dream—each stunning design aspect and creative detail brilliantly combining the venue's grandiose history with the needs of guests used to gold-standard customer service.

But as Katie tried to capture every detail, and file them away for future reference, her heart continued to clatter in her chest and her whole body throbbed, not from the event itself, but from the overwhelming experience of being Conall O'Riordan's date.

She had expected him to use the event for networking. After all, the people in attendance were surely his crowd, not hers? But he seemed almost bored with the proceedings, his attention focussed solely on her—and the comment he'd made earlier in the evening before leaving her at the door to her suite kept repeating in her head.

The emerald-gown constricted around her ribs every time his hand landed on the small of her back to lead her through the crowd. The bustier she wore—which had been so comfortable in the boutique that morning—all but cut off her air supply as they'd sat down to dinner. And his gaze had kept dropping to her lips while she'd nibbled at the array of rich, beautifully flavoured dishes, none of which she'd wanted to eat. Her nipples had squeezed into hard, swollen peaks as soon as he had arrived at her door to escort her down over four hours ago.

She felt both exhausted and energized, speechless and at the same time unable to stop talking, her nerves increasing the deep yearning sensation tightening her skin and making it impossible for her to focus on anything but him.

They danced together to the music of a full orchestra in the main ball room, the low lighting going some way to hiding her vivid blush as his hand trailed across the sensitive skin of her back where the gown dipped—sending the familiar riot of sensations deep into her sex.

At last, he drew her close to whisper against her earlobe, 'How about we call it a night?'

She nodded, not able to reply, her voice suddenly trapped somewhere around her solar plexus. It was a loaded question. They both knew where they would end up if they left the ball. The hunger in her abdomen tangled with the sudden spurt of panic and apprehension.

Should she have told him she'd never done this before? Did he have a right to know she might be terrible at it?

'Are you sure now?' he said, the husky Irish brogue thickening. He studied her face, waiting patiently for her answer, the amusement fading to be replaced by that focussed intensity that had unsettled her so much when they'd first met—

but which only made the heat swell and pound in her veins more fiercely now. 'I believe they have fireworks to come in the courtyard…' he added, his dark-blue gaze now so hot with purpose she imagined it sizzling over her skin. 'We can stay if you wish to see them.'

The ball wasn't due to end for another hour… at least.

'I don't want to wait…' she managed to whisper, her own voice so raw she didn't recognise it. 'And I really don't need any more fireworks,' she added.

He laughed, the sound gruff, but then stopped dead in the middle of the dance floor. The other couples glided past them, but her focus remained solely on him, now mesmerised by the heated purpose in his gaze. Almost as if in slow motion, he lifted her hand to his mouth, opened her trembling fingers and murmured something in a language she didn't recognise… Then bit softly into the swell of flesh beneath her thumb.

She jolted, the heat ricocheting through her over-sensitised body like an Exocet missile and exploding at her core.

'Let's get the hell out of here, then. I think we've waited long enough,' he murmured, his gaze never leaving her face.

She nodded.

The next ten minutes seemed to last several

eternities, her mind spinning through all the things that could go wrong tonight as he clasped her hand and led her off the dance floor. As he had done all evening, he dodged the greetings of famous people from politics, film and sport she recognised as they left the ballroom and made their way through the crowd back towards the hotel's private suites.

He took her up a dark staircase. She felt like Cinderella again, but this time she was running away with her prince.

Stop romanticising, Katie.

She tried to tell herself this wasn't a dream, it was reality, but still she struggled to focus on anything other than the pounding beat of her heart and the realisation the moment she had waited for so long was rushing towards her now at breakneck speed.

Was Conall O'Riordan really the right man? She still knew so little about him. And yet she trusted him. But did she trust him too much?

She was breathless and more than a little shaky when he shouldered open the door at the top of the staircase and she found herself in the corridor leading to their rooms.

His fingers squeezed hers, his hold both determined and reassuring as they arrived at the door to her suite. She stood dumbly for a moment, everything inside her clutching and releasing, the heavy weight in her sex almost as disturbing as her racing pulse.

'You'll have to open the door, Katherine,' he said, the lilt of amusement roughened by arousal.

She scrambled to find the key card in her clutch bag but her fingers were trembling too much to slide it through the slot. He took it from her, swished it through then handed it back.

'Thank you,' she said, tucking it back into the clutch.

'You're welcome,' he said, the rumble of humour only making her feel more gauche, more exposed.

Opening the door, he let her step inside. She stood on the carpet as he closed it behind them. The view of the City of Lights from the suite's stone terrace looked like a carpet of stars rolled out to the horizon.

But all she could concentrate on was him as he stripped off his tux jacket and approached her.

'Let me,' he said as he took her purse and dropped it onto a nearby chair, then ran his thumbs under the gown's jewelled straps.

She nodded, even though it wasn't really a question. Her breathing accelerated again as he brushed the straps off her shoulders and then found the zip under her arm. The bodice released, drooping down to reveal the lacy bustier. She drew in a jagged breath.

'Beautiful,' he said, tracing the soft swell of her cleavage above the lacy prison. Her ribs contracted, her nipples already begging for his touch.

Threading his fingers into her hair, he tugged her head back, his gaze—hot, demanding, hungry—roaming over her face.

He swore under his breath. 'The last four hours have been pure torture.'

The desperation in his tone spurred her senses. She flattened her palms against the rigid muscles of his abdomen and felt them tense against her seeking fingers beneath the starched shirt. He clasped her face in rough palms and covered her lips at last.

The kiss was forceful, demanding, as furious as the night before but so much more overwhelming. The fire at her core sparkled and glowed, spreading up to her breasts, down to her toes, making her shaky and desperate.

She tugged his shirt out of his trousers, needing to feel him. Her fingers touched his abs, exploring the velvet-soft skin rippling with strength.

He tore his mouth away, his breathing as hard and thready as hers. Then he stepped back to tug off his tie and rip open the shirt. Buttons popped, the violent action making her breathing ragged as he threw the shirt away.

The moonlight gilded the ridged muscles of his six-pack, the bulge of his pecs and biceps. Katie looked her fill as he unbuckled his belt.

He dipped his head to undo the zip and open his trousers to reveal tight black boxers moulded to the thick outline of his erection.

How is that going to work?

She blinked several times, the question only making her more giddy as she stared at the hard evidence of his desire.

'Hey.' He lifted her chin. 'Is everything okay?'

She nodded again. 'Yes, wonderful.'

'You've got too many clothes on.' He smiled that devastatingly intense smile that turned all her misgivings to mush.

Everything inside her tightened and pulsed.

The erection will fit and it will be wonderful.

She wanted him inside her. She wanted to know what it felt like to be possessed by a man. Especially this man. She'd waited long enough. Far too long, really.

He toed off his shoes and stripped off his trousers. Standing before her in only his boxers, he looked magnificent in the pre-dawn light.

Stepping back towards her, he clasped her neck and murmured against her lips, 'Your turn.'

She felt his smile as her own lips curved. He continued to kiss her, light, fleeting, hungry kisses across her nose, her chin and her neck, the rasp of his stubble livening up her skin as she struggled to get out of the dress with clumsy fingers.

'Do you need some help, Katherine?' he asked, the strained humour in his voice going some way to dispelling the embarrassment scorching her skin.

She nodded dumbly. Emotion welled in her throat when he dragged the gown off, then dropped to his knees. 'Let's handle the shoes first, *mo mhuirnín*,' he murmured.

She grasped his shoulder to steady herself as he slipped off one jewelled slipper. 'What does that mean?' she asked.

'Huh?' he said as he discarded the other shoe.

'Mu-voor-neen...' she replied, trying to pronounce the strange words.

He frowned, colour shadowing his tanned cheeks. 'Did I say that?'

'Yes', she said, wondering where the guarded look had come from.

'It's nothing, just some nonsense in Irish,' he murmured as he stood and turned her round to unhook the bustier.

She folded her arms over her breasts as the garment loosened, aware of her nipples tightening, the hard peaks clearly visible through the lacy fabric. She ducked her head, trying to hide her embarrassment. She'd never undressed in front of anyone before.

But as she faced him again, he touched her chin, nudging up her face. 'I've been wanting to see the rest of you ever since you were all but spilling out of this gown this morning.'

The small joke had a chuckle bursting out of her mouth. She let her arms drop, the bustier falling away. But the intensity, the sparkle of sensation, returned as he stripped off the last of her undergarments.

He swung her round again so she could see their reflection in the terrace doors. The hard ridge of his arousal pressed against her back as he traced her ripe nipples, plucking and playing with the taut peaks. Her head dropped against his shoulder when he covered her aching breasts at last, caressing, weighing the swollen flesh, his lips finding the pummelling pulse in her neck.

She gasped and bowed back, all her senses focussed now and yearning as one large hand slid down her torso and located the aching, tender, melting spot between her legs.

She sobbed, the spiral of need, of desperation, tightening, throbbing, so perfect it hurt as he found the slick, swollen nub with sure, certain fingers and circled it... So close and yet not close enough.

Teasing, torturing, tormenting.

He lifted her arm and draped it over his neck, leaving her open, her back arched, her breasts begging for his attention as he covered one turgid nipple, while one thick finger entered her and drove her wild.

'Please… I… Please…' She begged for the release which beckoned just out of reach.

'Shh, *mo mhuirnín*,' he said again, the endearment as raw and desperate as she felt.

Then he touched the very heart of her. His thumb flicked the spot where the heat gathered and pulsed. The orgasm cascaded through her, making her buck and moan, dragging out the pleasure in titanic waves of a release so strong, her knees gave way. She groaned as the last wave finally washed over her, retreating, leaving her limp.

He scooped her up and placed her on the couch. She watched, dazed, transfixed, as he kicked off his boxers, his hands as shaky as she felt.

The huge erection sprang up, long and thick, the swollen head glistening with moisture. Cursing, he scooped up his trousers again, found a small foil packet, ripped it open with his teeth and sheathed himself.

The emotion clutched in her chest again at the realisation that he had thought to protect her, when she'd been too lost in sensation, too dazed by need, to think of protecting herself.

She wasn't afraid any more, nor unsure. The yearning built again, swiftly and surely, her body clutching on emptiness, desperate to be filled.

Sitting down on the couch beside her, he dragged her up and over his lap until she knelt above him, her hands on his shoulders. He kissed her, his tongue possessive, demanding and, clasping her hips with firm hands, guided her onto the huge erection.

She sank down, the recent orgasm easing the way despite the stretched, full feeling. She ignored the pinch of pain, the fullness almost more than she could bear as she impaled herself to the hilt.

He swore softly and tugged her head back to stare into her eyes. 'Am I your first?' he demanded, his face a picture of need, hunger but also...something else, something she didn't understand. Was that shame? Shock?

She could have lied. A part of her wanted to—he did not look happy—but she knew she owed him the truth. Maybe she owed herself the truth. She wanted him to know he was the first man she'd ever trusted with this part of herself. And he'd already made it magnificent.

So, she nodded. 'Yes.'

* * *

No... Damn it.

Conall's mind screamed in denial. But it was already too late. He could feel the desire licking at his spine, impossible to deny a moment longer.

She was so hot, so tight around him. He had to move. Had to finish this now. It was too late to take it back.

He pressed his forehead to her chest, kissing the peak of one ripe nipple, then lifted her off him and placed her on the couch, his whole body clamouring now for release. She looked dazed, sweet, giddy and so brave. She had no idea what she'd just done. But it didn't matter now. It was too late to change.

He cupped her cheek. 'Tell me if it hurts.'

Surely it had to hurt? He was a large man, and she'd been so tight.

But she shook her head as he pressed inside. 'It doesn't, it feels good.'

He thrust into her, slowly, carefully, or as carefully as he could when his whole body was a mass of desperation.

Like their kiss the day before, and everything that had happened since, he could feel his control slipping but was powerless to stop it. Forced to move, inside the grip of her body, he thrust harder, faster, needing her to take every inch of him. The bad as well as the good.

He rocked out and back, the desire like a tsunami now, rolling through him, the approaching climax more powerful than any he'd ever felt before.

He found the slick nub of her clitoris, clumsy and desperate to make her go over first. Her muscles clenched as she sobbed out her release, bucking beneath him as the wave took her. He let go at last, everything he was, everything he believed himself to be, shattering as he soared.

But as he crashed to earth the last words his father had ever spoken to him echoed in his head—damning him.

'Women are the heart of us. Remember that and protect and respect them always. Do you promise me, lad? Never take what you can't give back.'

Katie lay sated, exhausted, her body limp and her mind a mess of fuzzy thoughts and emotions. Conall's head lay heavy on her shoulder, the erection still firm, still *there*, inside her. Their panting breaths filled the heady silence.

Her heartbeat battered her ribs as her breathing finally began to slow. She touched his cheek, stroking his damp hair back from his forehead with tender fingers. And tried not to lose herself in the swell of emotion making her chest hurt.

Only chemistry. And a marvellous adventure.

Just because he's your first, it doesn't make this more than sex.

He shifted, then lifted himself up. His gaze—assessing, intense and not entirely happy—searched her face. The expression in his eyes made no sense… She would have expected surprise, possibly even annoyance, because she hadn't mentioned her virginity. She'd realised her mistake as soon as he'd questioned her in that raw, shocked tone while buried deep inside her.

But he didn't look like that now… If anything, he looked…resigned? Did he regret what they'd done already? A heavy weight dropped into her stomach, but before she could say anything he rolled off her. And sat up.

'Conall, I'm sorry…' she said, confused now, as well as wary. Did it really matter that he had been her first? Surely her virginity was her business? It wasn't as if she'd set out to deceive him… And why should he even care? This was maybe a bigger deal for her than she'd realised. She hadn't expected her first experience to be quite so—well, so overwhelming, the passion and pleasure so intense or so intimate. But she doubted it could have been that intimate or overwhelming for him. Surely he was used to these sensations, more than aware of how transformative sex could be? He'd had girlfriends before her.

He glanced over his shoulder. 'Sorry for what, now?'

'For not telling you about…' The words came out on an embarrassed whisper. 'Well, about you being my first. I didn't think it would matter that much to you.'

'Uh-huh,' he said, then reached down to scoop up his boxers. He stood up to put them on, then walked off into the bedroom without saying anything, without even looking at her.

The bubble of panic pressed against her breast bone as she heard the toilet flush and the water run in the *en suite* bathroom. She imagined him getting rid of the condom and washing his hands. Then she waited.

Was he angry? Why?

Finally, he reappeared, wearing one of the hotel's plush bathrobes with another in his hand. He gave it to her. 'You best put this on, so we can talk.'

She tugged the robe on, grateful for the coverage, far too aware of all the places her body still burned from his focussed, forceful caresses. And how much it still yearned for his touch, despite the tenderness between her thighs. But even that felt more like an ache than a pain, an ache that was already eager to be filled again.

Who knew sex with Conall O'Riordan would make me insatiable?

The silly thought helped her to relax a little as he sat on the couch and beckoned her over. ‘Come here,’ he said. Gripping her fingers, he pulled her down to sit beside him.

He didn’t sound angry. Not exactly. But the look he sent her wasn’t really putting her at ease either. Because she had the strangest feeling he could see right into her soul at that moment. And that she was powerless to protect herself from that probing, oddly dispassionate gaze.

‘How come you’re a virgin if you were married?’ he asked.

The question came out of left field, making her think of Tom for the first time in all of this. The pulse of grief was there, but right behind it was the cruel stab of guilt.

Intellectually, she knew she had nothing to feel guilty about. She’d made her peace with Tom a long time ago. She had never considered taking this step until she was ready. She hadn’t betrayed her husband, because they’d never had that kind of a marriage, but still it felt like it would be a betrayal of the friendship she and Tom had shared to tell Conall the whole truth. So she attempted to tell him the lie she’d told herself all these years.

‘He was very sick when we got married. He c-couldn’t…’ She stammered to a stop as his eyes narrowed on her face and the flush of guilty knowledge heated her cheeks. 'It wasn't that type of…'

She cleared her throat and stared down at her hands, which were clasped so tightly in her lap the knuckles had whitened. She'd always been a terrible liar, unfortunately. 'He wasn't able to…' She stopped abruptly when his knuckle touched her chin and he raised her head, watching her again with that all-seeing gaze.

'*It* wasn't that type of marriage, or *he* wasn't able to? Which was it?' he asked, his tone calm but insistent, instantly picking up on the inconsistency in her statement.

She shrugged and looked away, the guilt now like a boulder in her throat. She'd lied to Tom, as well as herself. They'd lied to each other with their marriage. Perhaps it was time she admitted that. She drew in a steadying breath and twisted her fingers. 'Both, I suppose.'

He placed a hand over hers, rubbing his thumb over the skin. 'Explain it to me,' he said. 'Why did you marry the boy if you didn't want to sleep together?'

'Because he was dying, and he was my best friend,' she murmured. 'He didn't have anyone else. No family. And I didn't want him to be alone.' She sniffed and wiped her eyes with the sleeve of her robe.

And I didn't want to be alone either… The reality of what she'd done echoed in her head, clear for the first time.

'So you married him out of pity,' he said.

The stark truth sounded so harsh, so unforgiving, so childish and foolish when he said it like that. Shame thickened the guilt in her throat.

It was the same thing Ross had accused her of all those years ago. Back then, she'd been so angry with her brother. Annoyed that he would reduce what she felt for Tom to something so crass. She had convinced herself at the time that Ross was simply incapable of love himself, so he didn't understand it in others. She'd told him he was wrong, that what she felt for Tom was something he didn't understand. But she could see now, all too clearly, what she'd felt for Tom wasn't the kind of love which should have led to marriage, not even close.

And she wasn't even sure any more she'd done it for Tom's benefit. She'd been so determined. She'd wanted to make everything better, to give him something to live for, but she'd also been determined to prove her brother wrong. To do it in spite of his objections. And Tom had been stuck in the middle. All she'd really done was give him false hope and a fake marriage that had made *her* feel better about losing her best friend.

'I think I thought, if I married him, I could fix everything. That even if I couldn't make him better, I could make him happy.' She choked out a laugh that lacked any warmth or humour as she thought of Tom's words on their wedding night—how guilty she'd made him feel because he'd always known he couldn't be a real husband to her. 'God, I was so young. What the hell was I thinking?'

Conall squeezed her fist. 'Don't beat yourself up too much. There's no point in regretting things already done.'

She sighed. 'No, I suppose not.'

'And marriage is best without that nonsense about love anyway. At least you know that now, which'll make our situation a lot easier.'

She turned to him, shocked by the statement and the prosaic way he'd said it. And the indomitable look on his face. 'I don't understand—what has my marriage to Tom got to do with us?'

Especially as there wasn't really an *'us'*. Even if a tiny part of her heart pulsed at the thought there could be…there might be.

Terrific, now I'm delusional as well as insatiable.

'Not a lot,' he said. 'Except I think you should marry me now.'

CHAPTER TEN

'WHAT?' KATHERINE STARED at Conall as if he'd just suggested she jump off the balcony with him.

He had expected her to be surprised, had been ready for some push back. After all, they hardly knew each other. What he hadn't expected, though, was the blank look of absolute shock on her face.

But he'd given it some thought in the bathroom while calming himself down—after the tumultuous orgasm, the hideous reality of her virginity and the discovery of the risks he'd put her through—and it was the best solution. And the only way to honour the sacred vow he'd made to his father on his death bed not to exploit a woman's innocence.

At the time, his father had made him make the vow to protect his sisters and his mother. But how different was Katherine from them? She'd been abandoned by the same bastard—her half-brother—who had abandoned Carmel.

Plus, there were other more prosaic benefits to a union between them. He'd been thinking for a while now that a marriage would be a good business move as it would stabilise his personal life. Christy had put the thought into his head with her constant questions on the topic—but he'd discarded the idea because she wasn't the right candidate.

But, unlike Christy, Katherine was refreshingly low-maintenance. The only thing that had given him pause was the thought of her romanticism—the eager, artless, sweetness that had captivated him that afternoon could be a problem going forward.

But after talking to Katherine about the reality of her marriage he had become convinced she might be a good candidate after all. She'd already married one man for something other than love. She might be innocent when it came to sex, she might even love the trappings of romance, but she also understood marriage could be a prosaic, practical arrangement. They shared a rare chemistry which would no doubt fade in time, but until it did it could be a strong basis for their union. And she amused him. They'd had fun this afternoon, her quick wit and optimistic nature something he had enjoyed. That had to count for something, right?

The truth was, he had never looked for a grand passion in his relationship with women. Had never wanted it. He knew what that kind of devotion could lead to, and he wanted no part of it. But he'd also never really considered the possibility of friendship with the women he dated. He'd certainly never enjoyed a woman's company the way he had enjoyed Katherine's today—she had entertained him with her quick wit and artless sweetness and made him eager to explore so much more than just their incendiary chemistry.

Until this moment, he'd never considered marriage seriously, despite its obvious benefits to his business and personal life, because even the thought of it had bored him. He couldn't see himself getting bored with Katherine, though, unlike all the other women he'd dated.

'Are you joking?' she asked, still staring at him as if he'd lost his mind.

'Not at all. I took your innocence, Katherine,' he said with all the gravity he felt. 'That means something to me, something very profound.' He took her hand in his and covered her trembling fingers, even more sure that this was the right course of action. How was what he'd just done any different from what Ross De Courtney had done to Carmel? His sister had been seduced by Katherine's bastard of a half-brother—a man much more worldly than she was—and then discarded. The only real difference here was Conall hadn't *intended* to risk a pregnancy. But that didn't alter the fact there was still a reckoning to be paid.

'I made a vow to my father, on his deathbed, when I was a boy of sixteen, that I would protect the women in my life. I failed my sister Carmel.'

And my mother.

He paused, quashing the errant thought and the turmoil of emotions it caused. She didn't need to know how comprehensively he'd failed *all* the women in his life.

'I refuse to fail you too.'

'How did you fail your sister?' she asked, her wide eyes so full of concern, he found himself squeezing her fingers. Damn, how did she get to be so innocent, so compassionate, after everything she'd already been through in her life?

'You know how, I told you. She was only nineteen when she got pregnant. I refuse to be a man like the guy who seduced her. Ever. Do you understand?'

'But Conall…' She tugged her fingers out of his grasp, and he felt the loss immediately. 'I'm not nineteen, I'm twenty-four. And you didn't seduce me. I wanted to have sex with you…' Her skin lit with a vivid flush. 'Very much. And I'm not going to get pregnant because you had the good sense to use a condom, remember?'

'It split,' he said, and watched her skin pale.

'Oh,' she said, her throat contracting as she swallowed.

'In my haste to get the damn thing on, I must have punctured it. You'll be glad to know I've never been dumb enough to open the packet with my teeth before,' he said, because she had to know he'd hardly been celibate up to now. 'But pregnancy is a possibility. Unless you're using contraception?'

'I…' She swallowed again, her eyes widening to saucer-size, and he could see every emotion flit across her features—worry, guilt, regret, embarrassment. 'I'm not, no, but it's probably only a small chance.' She cleared her throat, the flush on her cheeks endearing despite the circumstances. 'I'm at the very beginning of my cycle.'

The blush turned the sprinkle of freckles on her nose to beacons. And he had the strangest realisation he was actually pleased he was the first man she had ever had such an intimate conversation with.

Neanderthal much, boyo?

Not a reaction he would have expected, but he decided to go with it. After all, everything about his interaction with this woman had been unexpected so far, and weirdly—given that he was a man who didn't usually enjoy unscheduled surprises—it was another thing about her he found fascinating.

'I could take emergency contraception,' she offered.

'If you wish, yes,' he agreed. 'But do you want to?'

He guessed on one level it made sense. And, truth be told, if he had ripped a condom with any of his other girlfriends his reaction would have been very different. But when he'd taken if off in the bathroom and realised the problem, the panic simply hadn't come. He hadn't felt trapped. Instead, the prospect of a pregnancy had seemed oddly inevitable, even fortuitous.

He'd already felt the weight of the vow he'd made to his father, the fact of her virginity determining what he had to do next to make amends. But, more than that, he'd been able to picture the child they might have, with his focus and her optimism, his drive and her compassion.

He adored Mel's son, Cormac. Family was a hugely important part of his life. It was the bedrock on which he'd built his empire. After his mother's death, he'd never shirked that responsibility, had never wanted to.

It was one of the reasons he had worked so hard to amass the fortune he had—more than any man could ever spend in a lifetime. Up until this point, he'd avoided the inevitable question of when or even if he planned to have children of his own. But as he'd examined the torn rubber and realised what had happened a strange calm had settled over him—at the thought the choice might already have been taken away from him.

Fate was a powerful thing, something he had always believed in—well, he was an Irishman born and bred, after all. And if fate had determined they should have a child, then so be it.

'I… Are you saying you don't want me to take emergency contraception?' she managed, the shock replaced by confusion.

He cupped her cheek and brushed his thumb across her lips, suddenly needing to touch her, to make this moment more tangible, more real.

'It is your choice, Katherine… But, honestly, I suppose I realised when I saw the condom had split I would not be averse to the prospect of a pregnancy.'

'But… *Really?*' Her voice came out on a squeak of shock. 'You're not upset? We've only just met, and we're not even dating properly…'

'We are now,' he said, just in case she was in any doubt. 'And, no, I'm not upset,' he said, a little surprised himself by how sure he was of that. 'Family means everything to me. And being a father is something I think I would be good at,' he added. 'After all, I've had quite a bit of practice already.'

Maybe he had made mistakes and dropped the ball with Carmel and his mother, mistakes he would always regret. But here would be a chance to make amends in so many ways.

'I don't know what to say,' she said with an honesty he had come to admire.

'I've given you a lot to think on, for sure,' he said, smiling at her perplexed expression. 'You don't have to make a decision tonight. You have time.' He glanced at the clock on the wall behind her head. 'I need to leave early in the morning—for a business trip to Australia. Let Liam know when you're ready to return to London—and he'll make all the arrangements.'

He stood, dragging her up with him. He brushed a curl behind her ear, trying to ignore the soft rise and fall of her breathing, the glimpse of cleavage and the desire to strip her out of the robe and take her to bed. There would be time enough for that when he returned.

'I won't see you in the morning, then?' she asked, sounding disappointed. The surge of possessiveness was swift and unequivocal.

'No.' He leaned forward and forced himself to brush his lips across her forehead rather than tasting her mouth. The shudder of response, the flash of arousal in her eyes, sent the inevitable shot of heat straight to his crotch. He forced himself to ignore it as he scooped his clothing off the floor. 'You've a week before I come back,' he said, knowing he would be unable to leave her alone longer than that, already stupidly eager to have her again. 'Which will give you time to heal. And consider my proposition.' He was rushing her, and he knew it, but he saw no reason to wait.

He strode out of the suite, leaving her silent behind him, already able to hear her mind galloping to keep up with him.

Good luck with that, Katherine.

He was a determined man—ruthless, successful and goal-orientated. Once he had set his sights on something, he never failed to achieve it. And he had just set his sights on Katherine Hamilton.

All he had to do now was get Katherine to agree to their union. Perhaps he couldn't offer her the romance she craved but he could offer her so many more tangible benefits—companionship, friendship, financial security and, of course, a chance to explore their spectacular chemistry.

He wasn't even bothered that she was Ross De Courtney's sister any more. He'd have to tell her eventually of her brother's connection with Carmel and Mac. But the bastard had abandoned her too, so she owed the man no loyalty whatsoever.

CHAPTER ELEVEN

'KATIE. OH. MY. GOD. You looked stunning yesterday. The pictures of you and the "Irish Bad Boy Billionaire" are all over the internet this morning. Why didn't you tell me you were going to the Lumière Ball? And that you're dating O'Riordan? What's he like? Is he as brooding and delicious as he—?'

'Hi, Caro.' Katie's face heated as she interrupted her best friend and top executive assistant Caroline Meyer's stream of consciousness long enough to hook her coat over the rack crammed into their tiny office in East London. 'How's everything been?'

The question was punctuated by the ring of the phone. Caro grabbed the handset on her desk because, as well as being her top executive assistant, Caro also doubled as their receptionist.

'Hi, Hamilton Events, Caro speaking, could you please hold?' she said, then covered the receiver. 'Are you kidding?' She grinned. 'The phones have been ringing off the hook ever since I got in two hours ago!'

Her face beamed with a combination of curiosity and excitement. 'O'Riordan's company account put it out on social media this morning that Hamilton Events is organising some top-secret family deal for him. And that's how you guys met. Ergo, we are now the go-to company for high-end event planning. Everyone who's anyone wants to hire us.'

She gave a deep sigh, hugging the phone to her chest. 'Honestly, it's actually like a fairy tale. You both looked so into each other. It's so romantic.' Another big sigh. 'And after only a week? Love at first sight really does exist.'

Except he doesn't love me.

'Oh, hi,' Caro added as she spotted the man who had walked in behind Katie.

'Caro, this is Jack Mulder, my new…um…' Katie hesitated, still not quite able to believe how her life had changed so much in the space of one tumultuous weekend.

'Bodyguard and driver, Ms Hamilton,' Mulder supplied with a friendly smile.

'Right. Yes.'

'You have a personal bodyguard and driver now?' Caro sounded as stunned as Katie had felt when she'd been introduced to her new professional shadow and his team after Conall's private jet had touched down at Heathrow.

She'd come straight from the airport after dropping off her luggage at her flat, keen to get back to some kind of normality. But Jack Mulder's presence wasn't the only thing making that impossible—her thoughts and feelings had been in turmoil ever since Conall had proposed marriage and insisted he was perfectly okay with an unplanned pregnancy.

It was probably a good thing she hadn't seen Conall this morning—after a sleepless night at the Lumière, the text she'd received from him on the plane had been disconcerting enough.

In transit/meetings for the next few days. Will call you at home Friday evening. Eight p.m. UK time. Liam is making necessary arrangements for your safety and will put you through to me if you need to get in touch. Con

At least she now knew what the second sentence had been about. Liam had informed her it wasn't safe for her to travel by public transport any more—and that Conall insisted on certain security measures being in place for all his close acquaintances.

While part of her had wanted to object when she'd been introduced to Mulder—because her safety wasn't *really* Conall's responsibility—another part of her had been deeply touched he'd gone to the trouble of arranging security for her.

Ultimately, she'd spent the long drive back to her flat from Heathrow with Mulder at the wheel, arguing with herself about her reaction. She needed to be careful not to be a total push-over. Conall's attention was overwhelming enough without her letting her own insecurities get in the way.

She'd always been a sucker for any kind of male attention, perhaps because she'd been denied it throughout her childhood. She'd already married one man for the wrong reasons. She mustn't fall into the trap of thinking Conall loved her simply because he clearly had a bit of a 'white knight' complex.

As a result, what should have been exciting news—that Conall's and her romance had inadvertently given her business the boost she'd been hoping and planning for for months—felt anything but. In truth, all it did was pile on more pressure and make her feel even more overwhelmed. Because this wasn't a real romance any more than her first marriage had been.

The sex had been spectacular, maybe a bit too spectacular, because she should have rejected Conall's proposal straight away. Instead of which she'd given him the impression she could be won over, that she could be as pragmatic and cynical as he was. And she knew she couldn't… Not least because, she was very much afraid, she already had more feelings for him than she knew what to do with.

Feelings which had to do with much more than the two spectacular orgasms he'd given her while she made love for the first time, or the cherished way he had made her feel by insisting he employ a driver-cum-bodyguard to keep her safe… And everything to do with the fierce passion in his voice when he'd spoken of his sisters, his family, the possibility of children and marriage.

She'd always wanted to have children too… always dreamed of having a family she could love unconditionally and who would love her unconditionally in return… Enough to know she wasn't going to take emergency contraception, even though it had to be the smartest option.

But the truth was, her decision to risk an unplanned pregnancy—however slight the possibility—with a man she hardly knew wasn't even the scariest thing about this situation. By far the most terrifying thing was the fact that when Conall had offered her marriage—had offered her a life with him—in that firm, practical, no-nonsense and defiantly anti-romantic tone, her foolish, unguarded heart had shouted 'yes'.

Not because he was a billionaire who could

turn her boutique business into the go-to company for high-end events. Not because he was the hottest—well, the only—lover she'd ever had. Not because he was sinfully handsome, wonderfully compelling and wildly charismatic, or even because she knew he most likely would make a far better father than her own father had ever been to her. But because she had done something really, really stupid over their one tumultuous weekend together.

She'd fallen in love with a man she wasn't sure was even capable of loving her in return. And, if that wasn't delusional enough, she was very much afraid she was already in danger of persuading herself she could make this work… That maybe Conall could learn to love her back if she just gave him a chance. She knew she wanted desperately to give him that chance, to give *them* that chance. Despite the fact that her cock-eyed optimism—that love could always find a way, despite all evidence to the contrary—and her belief in happy-ever-afters had left her devastated once before.

And she had no guarantees whatsoever it wasn't going to kick her in the teeth all over again.

CHAPTER TWELVE

'CONALL! YOU CALLED!' Katie's heartbeat leapt into her throat as her lover's face popped up in the video-chat app on her phone at exactly eight p.m. on Friday evening—then wanted to kick herself.

Why had she thought he might not call? And what was he going to want to talk about? Because, even after five days apart, she did not have a coherent answer for him yet. About anything.

She'd arrived home an hour ago, having worked her butt off all week handling the never-ending stream of new clients—which had thankfully helped deflect the constant playback of every detail of their twenty-four hours together in Paris. What had comprehensively failed to redirect her thoughts in the last week, though, was the constant calls and emails she'd had to field from all her friends and acquaintances enquiring about the new man in her life.

Once she'd arrived home, she'd veered between exhausted, excited and panicked as the time scheduled for their call had drawn closer. She'd also spent far too much time debating what to wear while she showered, and put on make-up, then took it off again, only to settle on brushed cotton PJs and bunny slippers.

Seductive, much?

'Of course I called,' he said, the deadly dimple appearing in his cheek as he flashed her a weary smile. He looked rumpled and even more gorgeous than usual, bright sunlight shining off his dark hair. 'I said I would.'

'Yes, yes you did.' And she'd discovered even on their short acquaintance that Conall was a man of his word. 'Where are you?' she asked.

'Take a look,' he said, then flipped his phone around. 'It's a place I own on the Gold Coast—kind of soulless, but better than staying in a hotel when you're battling epic jet-lag.'

She took in a luxury open-plan living area complete with a spotless state-of-the-art granite-and-steel kitchen. The view of an infinity pool and a wide, empty golden-sand beach fringed by palm trees—the summer sun sparkling off crystal clear water—visible through the glass wall at the end of the space was almost as breath-taking as Conall's face when it filled the screen again.

'It looks amazing,' she said.

'Come with me next time,' he offered. 'I'll teach you how to surf.'

'How do you know I can't surf already?' she asked, surprising herself with the teasing comment, pleased when she heard his rough chuckle. 'What time is it there?' she asked, trying to dismiss the spark of joy in her chest which always came when she made him smile.

'Too early.' He yawned and her galloping heartbeat slowed at the comforting domesticity of the moment. 'Liam tells me you've been busy?'

'Yes, very,' she said, then began to babble about all the new clients they'd taken on. Her words tumbled over themselves, the need to keep talking about inconsequential stuff suddenly paramount. But eventually she wound down, noticing that his gaze had dipped.

'What?' she asked, able to feel the heat in his perusal even from the other side of the globe, the familiar pulse and throb in her core no less intense than it had been five days ago, or every night since—when she'd woken up hot and sweaty, her sex slick and swollen, the memory of their one night together still so vivid.

'What are you wearing?' he asked, his voice having dropped several octaves.

She chewed on her lip, wishing now she'd opted for the thong and see-through negligee she'd momentarily considered buying for tonight's call. 'My PJs,' she managed, unable to hide the apology in her voice.

'Cute… Show me,' he said, the tone becoming even huskier. Apparently he was undeterred by her complete inability to dress appropriately for a late-night video call with her lover.

'They're not remotely sexy,' she said, almost as embarrassed now as she was turned on.

'I'll be the judge of that.'

She lifted the phone up to give him an arm's length view of her totally unsexy PJs. 'See what I mean?'

'Hmm… The flying pink pigs are kind of hot, actually.' His deep voice—playful and yet intense—rumbled through her over-sensitised body and gathered like a warm weight in her sex.

'Really?' she asked, and he laughed again, the sound as strained as it was sexy.

'Katherine, how do you feel about losing your phone sex virginity with me too?'

'Yes,' she whispered, the weight in her sex pulsing now, the command in his voice as unbearably hot as the wicked intent in his eyes.

'Are you sure? Because you're going to have to do exactly as I tell you. No hesitations?'

'I… Yes,' she managed around the lump of lust forming in her throat to match the boulder now jammed between her legs. 'I can do that.'

'Good girl,' he all but purred. He ran his thumb across his lips, as if considering his options. 'Find somewhere to prop the phone, so I can see all of you. You're going to need both hands for what I have in mind.'

After two frantic minutes, she managed to position the phone to his satisfaction and found herself lying down on the sofa, still wearing the fluffy PJs, the brushed cotton like sandpaper now against her skin.

How did he do that? How did he turn her into a mass of throbbing desperation with a single look, a simple command?

'As much as I love the pigs,' he said. 'We're going to have to lose them. Take off the pants first,' he murmured.

She did as he instructed, the purred words of encouragement only adding to the torment as she stripped off the pyjama bottoms, finally lying in front of him in her panties and the pyjama top.

She could smell the musty scent of the moisture flooding between her thighs. Could he see it? Did he know what he did to her? But what might have embarrassed her once only made the hot weight heavier when he spoke again.

'Now the top—unbutton it for me, *mo mhuirnín*,' he murmured, using the Irish word he'd used before in passion. 'Slowly,' he added, when her trembling fingers popped open two buttons in quick succession.

She tried to slow down, but the feel of his gaze was pure torture, her breath becoming ragged as she finished unbuttoning the top.

'Show me your breasts,' he said, the demand back in his voice. She brushed the sides of the top away to reveal her swollen nipples. The peaks pebbled into bullets of need under his commanding gaze, the slight draft from her windows like an arctic storm on her over-sensitised flesh. He swore softly, the curse word full of approval and passion.

'Do they hurt?' he asked.

'You have no idea,' she all but groaned, earning another rough chuckle, this one even more strained than the last.

'Play with them for me,' he demanded.

She rolled the stiff peaks between her fingers, caressing, pinching, aware of his dark gaze spurring her on. The hot centre of her sex swelled and throbbed, the slick bundle of nerves somehow attached to the hard peaks, so achy now she began to move on the couch, thrusting her breasts up, offering them to him, so desperate for his touch she entered another realm. His words of encouragement and demand were the only thing tethering her to reality, until she could almost feel his lips, firm and strong, unyielding and relentless, working their magic on her turgid breasts.

'Lose your panties. Do it now.'

She struggled out of her underwear, fully displayed now, and yearning, her whole body one throbbing bundle of need.

'Now stroke yourself where you need me the most.' His voice cut through the fog of sensation, the swell of desperation.

She dragged her fingers through the slick folds and found the swollen nub begging for release.

'Rub it harder, make it burn. But don't go over, not until I tell you.'

She arched her back, struggling to hold on, to hold back, her movements his to command like a puppet and its master. Her staggered breathing was the only sound.

She circled the sweet spot, delved, flicked right at the heart of her pleasure, drenched in desperation. The orgasm flickered so close, but just out of reach, as the torture increased.

She heard his grunts, knew he had to be

pleasuring himself too as he watched her, commanded her. Somehow the thought that she could devastate him the way he devastated her gave her a strange jolt of power, just as he groaned.

'Now, go over now!'

The command had the orgasm crashing through her, wave upon wave of harsh, painful pleasure. Too much and yet not enough.

At last she lay, limp, exhausted, shuddering, on her couch. Her galloping heart finally slowed, but her body remained raw, tender, uninhibited.

She heard the stunned curse and lifted her heavy eyelids, still too shattered to summon the energy to cover herself as his gaze coasted over her flushed skin.

He swore, sounding almost as dazed as she felt. 'That's the best phone sex I've ever had. You're a natural.'

She choked out a weary laugh, stupidly pleased. Perhaps in this much at least, they could be equals.

'Get some sleep,' he said, the tone still commanding, but maybe less sure of itself than it had been at the start of the call. Why she should take even more pleasure from that flicker of uncertainty than the virtual sex, she had no idea, but she did.

'You're gonna need it,' he added. 'Because I've decided to leave early. And, when I get to your place, I intend to keep you very busy, doing that for real.'

CHAPTER THIRTEEN

'WHERE ARE we going, Jack? I thought we were meeting Conall at the Opera House,' Katie said to her driver, all too aware of the buzz of anticipation.

Tonight was the four-week anniversary of the night she and Conall had first made love in Paris. And she still hadn't had her period. Not that that really meant anything, she told herself staunchly. Her cycle was often irregular. It wasn't uncommon for her to have a six-week gap between periods. Of course, she could totally put them both out of their misery at this point and just take a pregnancy test. But Conall hadn't asked her to. In fact, he hadn't even mentioned the prospect of a baby again, since he'd returned from Australia three weeks ago, so she'd decided to wait and see.

Every time they'd made love since—and they'd made love a lot—Conall had worn protection. It had made her feel both cherished and yet unsure of where he really stood on the prospect of a pregnancy. He wasn't pushing it, she'd decided, and neither should she, because she really wasn't sure where she stood either. They were still in the honeymoon stage of their relationship, and what a honeymoon stage it was.

After so many years of being unaware of her sexual needs, she'd discovered a side to her personality she hadn't even realised existed. A sensual, exciting, erotic, insatiable side which she had been satisfying to her heart's content at every available opportunity. But, more than that, for the first time ever she felt truly a part of a couple.

Her experience as Tom's wife had been so brief, and also so fraught with tragedy, there had been no time to simply be with him, to have normal conversations the way she did with Conall.

They talked about everything, from where they would spend their weekend—at Conall's eight-bedroom Grade-Two-listed Regency town house in Kensington, or her one-bedroom flat in Shoreditch—to whether they should cook in or eat out at one of the many sumptuous restaurants where Conall was a regular.

Her social life had also become turbo-charged, with Jack Mulder arriving at her office several evenings a week to whisk her off to some red-carpet event in London or Dublin, or even one spectacular evening in Milan, which Conall had asked her to attend with him. After some initial nerves—because she was used to organising events, not participating in them—she'd become almost as blasé as Conall about travelling in his private jet or helicopter, having her own driver or hobnobbing with stage and screen stars, political grandees, pop divas, sports heroes and assorted other famous faces. She was also getting accustomed to the intrusive attention of the paparazzi and the press.

But the best moments by far were the private moments she got to spend alone with Conall, just the two of them. They both had busy careers, so it always felt as if those few evenings they got to share together—usually in his house, not hers—were a rare and special gift.

She still hadn't got too much more information out of him about himself, but in some ways she didn't care. They were getting to know each other and all those big questions could wait. Just being with him and discovering the little things—such as that he could cook a mean Irish stew, liked to nod off after sex while wrapped around her and had an encyclopaedic knowledge of the film *Mean Girls* because his sisters had watched it on a loop in their teens—was more than enough for now.

'Mr O'Riordan asked that I bring you to the town house first,' Jack replied as the car headed past Kensington Gardens. Her chauffeur-cum-bodyguard, who had become a trusted friend, sent her a gruff smile. 'The opera doesn't start for over an hour.'

'Okay.' Katie smiled back, thrilled at the prospect of seeing Conall alone—for a whole hour. Her cheeks heated at the thought of what they could do in that time, especially as she hadn't seen him in two days, after he'd had to make an impromptu trip to Ireland without her.

The car pulled into the driveway of Conall's elaborate stucco-fronted house. She bid goodbye to Jack and jumped out of the car as soon as it stopped. As she rushed up the stone steps, the front door opened and Conall appeared in the doorway looking beyond gorgeous in the tuxedo he'd donned for the opera.

Her heart danced into her throat.

'Hey, about time. What took you so long?' Conall murmured, before she barrelled into him.

He huffed out a laugh as she wrapped her arms around him, absorbing the delicious smell of juniper and pine that clung to him—the well of emotion blind-siding her, along with the familiar spurt of heat. He drew her into the house's warmth and slammed the door behind her with his foot, before lifting her face to his. 'Good to see you too,' he said, before his mouth covered hers.

The kiss was deep and demanding, full of promise and need. Her hands explored the ridged muscles of his abdomen beneath the starched linen of his dress shirt as he cupped her bottom through her dress, the desire as sharp and desperate as always. But as her fingers found the buttons of his shirt, clumsily flicking them open, her hands desperate to touch his naked skin, he tore his mouth away and drew back, holding her trembling hands at arm's length.

'Hold on. We're going to have to take a rain-check until after the opera,' he said, his pure crystal-blue eyes fixed on her face—the flare of passion contradicting the strained smile.

'Why?' she said, unable to hide her devastation.

He let out a gruff laugh. 'No pouting, Little Miss Ravenous.' His thumb skimmed over her bottom lip. 'I've got something for you.'

Threading his fingers through hers, he led her into the library off the main hallway. The musty smell of old leather and lavender polish filled the room.

'Sit down,' he said, and let go of her hand. After crossing the room, he clicked the dial on the safe built in to the shelving then produced a small velvet box.

Katie's heartbeat bounced back into her throat, her gaze fixed on the box as he walked towards her then knelt in front of her.

'Conall?' she whispered, so stunned she could hardly breathe, let alone talk or think coherently.

He hadn't mentioned marriage again, not since their first night in Paris. She'd simply assumed he'd changed his mind. But when he flipped open the box, to reveal a vintage ring studded with diamonds, her breathing stopped altogether, trapped somewhere around her diaphragm.

He touched her chin, lifted her startled gaze to his face then ran his thumb down her cheek.

'Breathe, Katherine,' he murmured in that husky voice that had the power to make her ache, and she suspected always would. He took the ring out and discarded the box, then lifted her trembling fingers with his other hand.

'It's my mother's ring,' he said. 'I went to Ireland to collect it, and to check with Immy and Mel they were okay for me to have it.'

'You did?' she said, still so stunned, she had to force herself to breathe before she passed out.

She hadn't yet met his sister Mel, or indeed his young nephew Cormac. And while she'd developed a great relationship with Imelda—the younger woman apparently overjoyed her brother was finally dating a 'real woman'—her words, not Katie's—the idea that he had discussed their marriage with his sisters felt huge. Too huge in a lot of ways.

'Uh-huh. I'd like you to wear it, as I want to marry you, Katherine.'

'But…' Her hand instinctively roamed to her stomach, her mind racing to catch up with her staggered breathing.

When he'd first proposed marriage it had seemed like a kneejerk suggestion. Something she hadn't really considered seriously since. Partly because it would have been far too easy to allow her romantic heart to say yes when it felt like the wrong thing to do. He had told her he didn't love her and had made a point of saying he didn't even think love was necessary in a relationship. But since then, her feelings for him had become so much deeper. She knew now this relationship was about more than just sex. But was it still too soon? Especially as she still couldn't be sure he wasn't doing this out of a sense of duty, a sense of responsibility. She knew he cared about her, he'd shown it in so many ways in the last month, but…

'I might not be pregnant, Conall,' she managed, trying to gauge his reaction. Was that the real reason he was asking? Because he thought he had to, after what had happened to his sister? 'I should have taken a pregnancy test.' Why the heck hadn't she? 'I can take one tomorrow. Then we'll know for sure if…'

'Shh…' He touched his finger to her lips to silence the panicked stream of words. 'This isn't to do with the possibility that you might be pregnant,' he said, covering the hand she had on her belly with his. The gesture had her heartbeat slowing to a crawl. 'As I said, I've no fear of fatherhood, would welcome it, in fact. I'm not getting any younger,' he added with a rough laugh that belied the serious expression. 'But this is about you and me. I want you to be my wife.'

She released a shuddery breath. The panic retreated to be replaced with something even more disturbing… *Hope.*

'But… *Why*, Conall?' she forced herself to ask.

He frowned, as if the question made no sense to him, then stood up, the ring in his fist as he paced away from her, then back again.

'Because we suit, Katherine. Surely it's obvious?' He ran impatient fingers through his hair. 'I can't keep my hands off you and, even when we're not tearing each other's clothes off, I like you. You're good company, funny, sweet, compassionate. And most of all smart and independent. This past month has proved to me we'll make an excellent team.'

It was hardly the declaration of love she might once have dreamed of, but then she knew that Conall was a practical, pragmatic man. And it wasn't really his words that mattered, she realised, but the emotion behind them. His agitation, impatience and the frustrated frown were somehow more compelling than the beautiful ring still clutched in his fist.

'And…' He knelt in front of her again and took her hands in his, his gaze so hot and determined she could feel her heart punching her chest and her resistance crumbling. 'And if we should be blessed with children. Now,' he added, glancing at her belly, 'or in the future, I know you'll make a good mother. You're strong, which is important, because sometimes motherhood can be so tough. My own mother struggled—' He stopped abruptly and looked away, the colour highlighting his cheeks making the emotion swell in her throat.

'Conall? What were you going to say?' she asked softly as he swore under his breath and got back to his feet.

He'd never spoken about his mother. All she knew was that Maeve O'Riordan had died a scant two years after her husband. Over the last few weeks, on the rare occasions when they'd spoken about anything personal, he had talked freely about his father. Enough for Katie to know Ronan O'Riordan had been a hugely important figure in Conall's life. She knew how much Conall had looked up to his father, how much he had respected and admired him—and how traumatic Ronan O'Riordan's sudden death in a farm accident had been for his only son, even though Conall seemed unwilling or unable to acknowledge that trauma himself.

But Conall's relationship with his mother had remained a mystery until this moment. Katie hadn't pressed him to talk about her. She knew how harsh unresolved grief could be, especially if your relationship with the person who had died was problematic. After all, she'd had to come to terms with her own issues with her mother after her death. Forced to acknowledge that in many ways Cathy Hamilton had always been more dedicated to her art than she ever had been to providing a secure and stable home.

'Nothing,' he murmured. But she could see it wasn't nothing. The colour highlighting his cheeks was so unlike him, she knew there was much more to his proposal than he had let on. This wasn't just about practicalities or great sex, or even the companionship they'd shared over the last few weeks.

Was it possible Conall might actually need her, in a way she already knew she needed him? The pounding in her ears became deafening.

She placed her hand on his arm. 'Conall, you do know you can trust me, don't you?' she said softly.

'I don't want to talk about it,' he said, sounding

frustrated, but also unsure of himself—which wasn't like him at all.

'I understand,' she said, determined not to push or be hurt by his denial. But when she dropped her hand from his jacket sleeve, he grasped her wrist to pull her closer.

'No, you don't,' he murmured.

He searched her face and ran his thumb down her cheek, the turmoil in his expression totally transparent for the first time since she'd met him. She knew he always held himself back, in a way she never had, but her lungs constricted, shocked by what she saw. Not just grief, and sadness, but also guilt and shame.

'She killed herself,' he said, the turmoil in his eyes as vivid as the confusion in his voice. 'Left my sisters and me, because she couldn't stand to live without him. She was always so fragile…' He let her go and stood up, his voice so full of pain now she could feel it tearing at her own composure.

'She miscarried two babies between having me and my sisters. I think it destroyed a part of her. And he always made allowances for that. Some days she couldn't even get out of bed, so he would do it all. I asked him once why he put up with her moods and he slapped me across the face for saying such a thing about my mother. It was the only time he ever hit me.'

He sat down heavily on the couch and sunk his head into his hands, running his fingers through his hair. 'He loved her so much, he forgave her everything. And I never understood it.'

Katie knelt in front of him. She placed her hands on his knees, her ribs squeezing at the shame and confusion on his face when his gaze met hers.

'I miss him, every day. But I don't miss her, even though I know the depression wasn't her fault,' he said so simply, her heart hurt. 'If that's what love does to you, I want no part of it in my marriage. If that's what you need from me, I can't give it to you.'

He opened his fist to reveal the beautiful ring nestled in the centre of his palm, the diamonds having reddened the skin where he had gripped it too tightly. 'This ring is probably cursed—why didn't I realise that?' he murmured, sounding so lost her heart broke—for the young man, not much more than a boy really, who had lost so much, so quickly and had never had the time and space he'd needed to come to terms with his loss.

Love wasn't about weakness, she thought. It was about strength. It couldn't heal depression or mental illness, but it could heal a heart. And it wasn't something you received but something you gave. His father had understood that, and so did he, even if he didn't realise it—or why would he have worked so hard to keep his family together after his parents' deaths?

But she couldn't tell him any of that, she realised. All she could do was show him.

And suddenly she knew she loved him. For better *or* for worse, and even if he didn't love her back… *Yet*… Some day he would surely take that leap too? Because he was more than capable of it.

He was terrified right now of feeling that deeply again, for anyone other than his father, his sisters and even his mother, but she could wait for those feelings to grow.

She cupped his jaw, the zing of awareness never far from the surface as his stubble abraded her palm and his gaze lifted.

'I'd love to wear her ring,' she said simply.

His frown deepened, but then the heat, hunger and something that looked very much like triumph turned his gaze to fire. 'You'll marry me?'

'Yes,' she whispered.

He gripped her neck, dragged her to him and devoured her mouth with a hunger and purpose that made her heart slam into her breast bone.

Standing up, he lifted her with him and growled. 'Put your legs around my waist. We're going to be a late for the opera.'

In the end they were close to an hour late for the opera. Conall had made himself drag Katherine out of bed—even though he'd never been that keen on opera, he knew she loved it, and he was scared if they had stayed in bed he might never want to leave it.

The hunger that had controlled him for over a month hadn't abated one bit. He'd had to force himself to leave London without her this week, after ignoring his businesses around the globe for three whole weeks—ever since he'd raced back from Australia two days ahead of schedule just to be with her.

He had hoped, once he got his ring on her finger, the driving hunger would begin to fade… No such luck, he realised as he showed her to her seat in their private box and watched her eyes glitter with emotion as the soprano on stage hit a stream of fanciful notes.

His fiancée wore a blue satin dress that skimmed her thighs, her curly hair still sexily rumpled from their love-making. How could she be even more beautiful every time he looked at her?

As he seated himself, his gaze snagged on the ring he'd placed on her finger. Why had he blurted out all that stuff about his mother?

And why had she accepted it all so readily?

He sat through the remainder of the opera's second act, the urge to skim his hand under her dress and touch her, taste her again, fizzing in his veins.

Why was the longing to be with her still so intense? To be near her? To brand her as his the only way he knew how at every possible opportunity?

It was madness. And he had a bad feeling it went way beyond their extraordinary chemistry. Or the practical benefits of a marriage between them. And had everything to do with the wide-eyed look on her face—so open, so unguarded, so full of hope—when he'd told her what he could never offer her and she had agreed to marry him regardless.

He'd known in that moment, Katherine had persuaded herself he could be the man she needed, the man she wanted, when he knew he could not. He should have told her the truth, made her understand that deep down he wasn't worthy of love, would never be worthy of love. Because he couldn't give it back.

He'd failed his mother, blaming her for something that had never been her fault, never realising how bad the grief had hit her until it was too late… And he would fail Katherine too—because he would never be able to open himself to that kind of pain. But he hadn't been able to say anything, because he'd wanted her bright, lively, compassionate presence in his life so much.

She glanced at him and smiled, applauding the performers as they left the stage and the theatre began to empty for the intermission.

'Well, at least we didn't miss the *whole* of the first half.' She grinned.

'Come on.' He stood and offered her his hand. He needed to get out of their box before he got ideas about kissing her again, because that way lay more madness—and possible arrest. 'Let's get a drink.'

After leading her through the crowds, they entered the exclusive private members' bar reserved for the people who owned the boxes.

'How about champagne?' he asked, keen to celebrate their engagement.

He was being an idiot. She'd agreed to marry him. Why was he complicating this? They would make a good team. There might even now be a child growing in her womb… He needed to tell her about her brother's connection to his family, but that could wait until after the wedding—which he planned to expedite as quickly as possible. He wanted her in his home, wanted his ring on her finger and his name on her passport.

She nodded, the blush lighting the sprinkle of freckles he had come to adore over the past four weeks, but as he lifted his hand to signal the barman her face paled as she spotted someone over his shoulder.

'Ross?'

He swung round to see a tall man standing behind him with a woman on his arm. She looked vaguely familiar, but it was the man's face that drew his attention, the shock of recognition going through him like a bullet.

'I didn't know you like the opera.' Katherine's distressed whisper came from a million miles away, muffled by the fury thundering in his ears.

'I don't,' the man said, the rigid muscle in his jaw softening as he stared at Katherine. But then he blinked, recovering himself. 'Katie, you look… Well…' The man's blue-green eyes, so like his nephew's, landed on Conall, his lips twisting in a caustic smile. 'Hello—O'Riordan, isn't it?' he said curtly, the conversational tone belying the focussed gleam in his eyes, as if he were assessing Conall's suitability to date his sister.

Conall's fury started to choke him. Who the hell did this bastard think he was?

'I saw in the press that you two were dating.' The man held out his hand towards Conall. 'I'm Katie's brother,' he added. 'Ross De Courtney.'

'I know exactly who you are.' Conall ground out the words. He glanced down at the offered hand, then shoved his own hand into his pocket.

His fingers curled into a fist as he grasped hold of the last thin threads of his control to stop himself from ploughing his fist into the bastard's face.

'You do?' The man's brow wrinkled, the muscle in his jaw working overtime now. 'Have we met?'

'Thankfully, no,' he said. 'But I know what a bastard you are.'

'Conall?' Katie gasped beside him, clearly shocked by his rudeness, but Conall didn't care. How dared this man call himself her brother? He had no right.

And how dared he look at Conall as if he weren't good enough to date his sister, when *he* was the one who had failed her so spectacularly?

'What's wrong?' Katie asked, confused now, the concern in her voice making the anger in his gut twist into something a great deal more volatile.

He should have told her, he realised. Long before now. Told her that Ross De Courtney was the bastard who had seduced and abandoned Carmel. But it was too late for explanations now. All he cared about was keeping this man the hell away from her. Because he'd seen the surprise in Katherine's face a moment ago, swiftly followed by the soft glow of pleasure. She was ready to forgive the bastard, a man who hadn't spoken to her in years, who had never been any kind of a brother to her, by the sounds of it. Because she was too soft-hearted, too sweet, compassionate and kind.

Which is the same damn reason she's willing to marry you. When you can't love her.

He dismissed the sickening thought. And forced his righteous fury with De Courtney to the fore to cover the wave of shame that followed hot on its heels. Maybe he couldn't love Katherine, but he would protect her from her bastard of a brother.

'Stay away from her,' he snarled, unable to recognise his own voice. 'You've no right to talk to her.'

'What the...?' De Courtney swore viciously, shock wiping the cynical smile off his face. 'Who the hell are you to tell me that?'

'I'm the man who's going to marry her.' Conall spat the words, his fist flexing.

The thundering in his head began to clear, though, as he became aware of Katherine's fingers digging into his other arm. And he looked down to catch the sparkle of diamonds on her finger.

'Conall?' He turned to see horrified shock tempered by the sheen of moisture in her eyes. 'What's going on? How do you know Ross?'

She blinked, the moisture sparkling in her eyes crucifying him.

He took her hand in his, suddenly desperate to get away, to get out, the shame rising up again to choke him. 'We should leave,' he managed around the brutal knot forming in his stomach. 'We need to talk.'

'Katie, don't be an idiot, the man's obviously insane,' came the brittle comment from her brother.

Conall stared at her, the urge to punch De Courtney all but consuming him now, but he held on to the fury as the shame in his stomach curdled to sick dread.

De Courtney didn't matter. What mattered now was getting Katherine out of here, so he could explain. Even though he wasn't even sure himself any more what he was supposed to say… Because this all suddenly felt like so much more than he'd ever meant it to be. So much more than he knew how to deal with. Because he hadn't been thinking about Carmel, or little Mac a moment ago. All he'd been able to think about was protecting Katherine. And that made no sense.

She glanced at her brother, but when her gaze returned to his, his heart galloped into his throat, the absolute trust he saw in her eyes crucifying him all over again. 'Okay,' she said. 'Let's go.'

He led her out of the bar, ignoring Ross De

Courtney behind them calling them both lunatics. But, as he gripped her hand, his galloping heart began to choke him… And the pain in his chest became so real and visceral, it terrified him.

CHAPTER FOURTEEN

KATIE SHIVERED, WRAPPING her arms around her stomach, trying to hold the shattered pieces of herself together as Conall's car drew up to the kerb outside the Opera House.

She'd left her coat in their box, she thought inanely, but it wasn't the winter wind, bitter against her skin, that had the cold wrapping around her heart.

'Here, you're freezing.' Conall's coat covered her shoulders, his strong arm banding around her waist to direct her into the car as Jack Mulder opened the passenger door.

The familiar scent of juniper and pine invaded her senses, but the inevitable rush of sensation from the warmth of his body heat that clung to the fabric refused to close the chasm opening up in her chest.

She sat stiffly in the seat, her movements somehow no longer her own, as if she were acting on autopilot.

A part of her knew she was in shock. The look of pure, unadulterated rage contorting her fiancé's face into someone she didn't recognise, as he'd confronted her brother and said what he'd said, replayed over and over in her head.

'I know exactly who you are.'

How did Conall know her brother? Why hadn't he said anything?

The truth was, she'd been considering contacting Ross ever since her conversation with Conall in Paris. She knew he lived in New York now, and she had even gone so far as to get his contact details. Their estrangement was stupid, she'd decided, a product of their foolish pride. She could see now he'd objected to her marriage to Tom to protect her. She was the one who had pushed him away, not the other way around, refusing to speak to him until he recanted—which of course he'd refused to do, because he'd never been very good at admitting he was wrong.

All those thoughts and feelings had been rushing through her head at breakneck speed but, before she'd had a chance to voice any of them, Conall had intervened.

And now the only word that kept racing through her mind was…*why?*

Where had that rage come from? He'd made it sound as if it had something to do with her relationship with Ross. But how could it, when they'd hardly spoken about their pasts? And he'd certainly never asked her any questions about her relationship with her brother.

The car sped through the evening traffic in Covent Garden as Conall placed his hand over hers, gathered her fingers and squeezed.

'I'm sorry,' he said, but the words sounded brittle, unconvincing, forced, said out of necessity rather than apology.

She glanced down at their joined hands, noticing the ring she had accepted so readily, so eagerly, only hours before on her finger.

She tugged her hand out of his, placed it in her lap and stared out of the window. Christmas decorations adorned the shop fronts along Piccadilly—expensive gold and silver satin bows, sprigs of lush red holly, lavish green pine boughs all lit by swathes of colourful fairy lights—as the car drove past Fortnum and Mason, the Wolseley, the Ritz. But what had enchanted her on the way to the theatre did nothing to lift the leaden weight in her chest now.

'How do you know my brother?' she asked dully.

The silence in the car stretched tight, the pain in her stomach becoming agonising as she waited for his answer. She forced herself to look at him and saw the flicker of indecision.

'Please don't lie. And tell me that was about

me,' she managed round the weight that had somehow risen up to jam itself into her throat.

The intensity of his gaze seared her skin, but she refused to look away, refused to break eye contact. Finally, resignation and regret shadowed his eyes.

'Your brother is the bastard who got my sister Carmel pregnant four years ago…' he said in a voice low with fury.

Katie sucked in a torturous breath, surprised she could still be shocked, but she was. Not just by his words, but the chilling anger in his eyes.

And in that moment a slew of memories came tumbling back. His words, his actions over the last month right from the first moment she'd met him, which she had interpreted one way—excused them in her ignorance and naivety, and forgiven them so easily in her determination to see the best in him, in *them*. But those words and actions looked so different now, the actual motivation behind them revealed in the cold, harsh light of reality.

'That's why you hired me?' she murmured, barely able to breathe now around the catastrophic weight pressing down on her chest. 'Why you made everything so hard for me. Why you invited me to Paris…'

'Maybe at first. I persuaded myself it was about him, but then…'

He stopped and stared down at his hands. But when he reached out to run his thumb down her cheek, as he had done so many times before, she reared back.

'Katherine, don't…' he murmured, his tone as broken as she felt. 'He's not why I…'

'Yes, he is,' she said. That brutal feeling of inadequacy that had dogged her throughout her childhood and adolescence—every time her mother hadn't seen her, every time her father had refused to acknowledge her, every time Ross had pushed her away, even when Tom had died when she had wanted so much for him to live—all came tumbling back.

'*He's* why you seduced me, why you wanted to marry me. It was all about him, wasn't it? You wanted revenge for your sister and your nephew, and I was it.' She was struggling to breathe now, the tears scoring her cheeks as she gulped in each painful breath.

Because she was that small, insignificant child again. The one no one had ever really wanted. She'd worked so hard to lose that girl, to be her own woman. She'd built a business, had stayed strong even after losing her best friend and had been prepared to give everything she was to Conall, but it had never really been her he wanted.

'That's nonsense, Katherine,' he said, and tried to reach for her again.

Her back slammed against the car door as she shifted away from his touch. She hit the button to open the driver's partition. 'Jack, stop the car. I need to get out.'

'Miss, is something wrong?' Jack glanced back, his voice concerned and wary.

'Stop the car, Jack,' Conall said.

As soon as the vehicle stopped moving, she jumped out. Hearing the door slam behind her, she raced forward, then turned to see Conall approaching her, his palms up. He looked concerned, probably because she was behaving like a crazy lady. She swallowed down the wellspring of emotion, knowing she had to deal with these feelings, had to find a way back—but she couldn't do it with him there, and that hurt, more than anything else about this whole mess. Because she loved him so much, and he had never loved her.

'Katherine, calm down please. Let's talk about this. I want you to be my wife.' His gaze dipped to her belly. 'Even now you could be pregnant with our child.'

The comment was like a body blow. Oh God, was the child he had said he wanted all part of this too? She shook her head. No, she couldn't think about that now.

'Did you ever love me, even a little bit?' she asked, her voice breaking on the pitiful plea.

He tensed, as if she'd hit him. And the catastrophic weight seemed to implode, bleeding its misery into the deep well of sorrow in the centre of her chest.

How could she have been so foolish? So misguided? God, he'd even told her he could never love her, and she hadn't listened.

She grasped the ring on her finger, twisted it off and held it out. 'You can take it back. I don't want it any more.'

Instead of taking it, he planted his fists in his pockets and stared at her. 'I won't take it. Not until you get back in the damn car and listen to reason.'

A part of her wanted to throw the ring at him, to match his anger and impatience with her own. But the twisting pain inside her was too draining even for anger now. So she placed the ring in the pocket of his jacket, took the garment off and dropped it onto the pavement.

'You're not listening to me, Conall,' she said with all the strength she could muster. 'I can't be your wife any more. Because I love you. And it's very clear now, you can never love me.'

She hesitated, giving him a moment to contradict her, but he said nothing, and her heart finally shattered into a thousand tiny pieces.

'If there's a child, we can discuss visitation rights through lawyers,' she managed. 'But I never want to see you again.'

She forced herself to turn and walk away from him. To hail a cab and climb in, drawing on the last reserves of her strength to tell the cabbie her address.

But as the taxi sped off, and she watched Conall staring after her, his discarded jacket in his hand, she knew she was lying to herself as well as him.

And when she sent him a text two days later, to tell him she'd started her period and there would be no child, her heart was still in bits and the agony was only more overwhelming.

Because she still wanted him, and the life she had believed they could make together, even though none of it had ever been real.

CHAPTER FIFTEEN

Two weeks later

KATIE DROVE THE small hire car along the driveway and gulped down the inevitable lump in her throat as Kildaragh Castle appeared—the glorious peaks and turrets highlighted by the cold December sun. As she braked in front of the main entrance, and spotted the path down to the secluded cove where she had once watched Conall battle the surf every afternoon, her breathing accelerated. The twin tides of panic and bone-deep sadness—a sadness she wasn't sure she'd ever be able to shake—was all but destroying her.

He won't be here. Imelda promised.

She sat in the car, taking several moments to regain her composure and some semblance of her usual professionalism.

The wedding was in two days' time, and Imelda had begged her to come and oversee the last of the preparations. After her split with

Conall, Katie had arranged to have the rest of Imelda's wedding arrangements handled by a well-respected wedding planner in Galway who had jumped at the chance to take on the prestigious commission.

Stepping out of the car, she picked up the folder that contained the final checklist she'd done to reassure Imelda everything was going to go brilliantly the day after tomorrow. The guests were due to start arriving this afternoon, so she'd left London on a five a.m. flight, determined to put Imelda's mind at ease and leave as quickly as possible.

It wasn't the pre-dawn wake-up call, the mostly hassle-free journey to Knock or the drive down the coast to Kildaragh, though, that was causing the fatigue dragging her steps as she headed towards the chapel where she and Imelda had agreed to meet. She'd barely slept in the last two weeks, her dreams as well as most of her waking moments filled with memories of him—some hot, others painful, all devastating.

Stop thinking about him. It won't help.

She berated herself for about the five thousandth time in the last fourteen days. Running through every second of their relationship wouldn't change the inevitable outcome or make her feel less of a gullible fool. He'd hurt her, yes, but she'd let him, and she had to take responsibility for that.

She pushed open the heavy oak door to the chapel and walked down the aisle, already expertly decorated with green satin ribbons and the beautifully arranged sprays of winter blooms she'd helped design with a local florist. *Before.*

'Hi, Imelda, it's Katie!' she shouted, glancing at her watch to check she wasn't early. 'Are you here?'

The musty interior was cool and dark, overlaid with the scent of roses and jasmine, shards of coloured light from the magnificent stained-glass window she had once admired lighting the dust mites.

'She's not, no.' The low reply ripped through her consciousness—stiffening her spine and making her heart slam into her breastbone.

She spun round to see Conall's broad silhouette standing in the vestibule behind her, before he stepped into the light.

Her heart stuttered, then stampeded.

He looked the same, and yet not. His usually expertly styled dark hair was in disarray, and the thick stubble on his jaw had become a beard, but when those pure blue eyes locked on her face the familiar jolt returned.

She dropped her folder, her whole body starting to shake.

'What are you doing here? Imelda p-promised…' she stammered. 'She said you would be in Rome,' she rambled, not sure she was making any sense, her heart beating so fast now it was gagging her.

She couldn't do this again. She didn't want to.

'She lied,' he said, walking towards her, his steps cautious but unrelenting, as if she were a wild animal he was determined to tame. 'I asked her to lie, to get you here. So I could talk to you.'

'No, I can't…' She shook her head, feeling the tears she'd already shed so many of stinging her eyes again.

It would break her.

But as she went to dash past him he grasped her upper arms in gentle hands to prevent her escape. 'Don't run from me again, Katherine, please.'

She braced her forearms against his chest and balled her hands into fists, struggling against his hold. The lungful of his scent—juniper, pine and clean citrus soap—making her frantic. He'd held her hopes and dreams in his hands and he'd crushed them. She wasn't strong enough to survive that again.

'Please, let me explain, let me apologise… There's so much you don't know, so much I should have told you.' The agony in his voice pierced through the fog of panic, and her struggles turned to shudders of anguish and grief.

'Katherine,' he murmured, letting go of her arms to cup her cheeks and lift her face into the light. 'You look shattered. Did I do that too?'

She could hear the devastation in his voice, see the harrowing regret in his eyes. She tugged her head out of his hands and wrapped her arms around her body, to hold onto all she had left… Her pride.

'It's okay,' she said. 'I'll be fine,' she managed, trying to salvage the last remnants of her dignity and stop the shaking.

'It's not okay, none of this is okay,' he said, thrusting his fingers through his hair. His shoulders slumped as he stepped back to give her space, and it occurred to her for the first time how shattered he looked too—as she noticed the bruised smudges under his eyes, the lines around his mouth, and the unkempt appearance, which was so unlike him.

She stifled the foolish kernel of hope that he had been as devastated by their parting as she had. Because how could that be true? And did it really make any difference? He'd lied to her, about everything.

'I ruined it because I didn't trust my own feelings,' he said, his voice, barely a whisper now, echoing in the old church. 'I want to explain,' he offered. 'But I don't want to hurt you any more,' he added. 'I guess I shouldn't have tricked you into coming here, but I was desperate. And I knew the stuff I wanted to tell you couldn't be said over the phone or via email.' He stepped aside and shrugged, the sincerity in his eyes making her heartbeat stutter and her stomach hurt.

He wasn't the charismatic, compelling man she had persuaded herself she had fallen in love with, but someone who was as confused and unsure as she was right now. He lifted a weary arm, presenting the door to her. 'If you need to leave, if you don't want to hear what I have to say, I won't stop you.'

Her body stilled as she searched his face. The glimmer of irrepressible hope, though, was somehow as painful as the devastation that had gone before. But then something twisted inside her, and suddenly she knew he wasn't the only one to blame for the mess they'd got themselves into.

She'd put him on a pedestal, allowed her romantic imagination to take over. Had she ever really looked at him for who he really was, instead of who she wanted him to be? Ever really admitted to herself the mistakes she'd made too? She'd rushed into this thing—had become addicted to the glamour, the excitement, the spectacular sex and the sheer adrenaline rush of being with him, being wanted by him—and had never stopped to ask herself what she needed, what she deserved.

She sighed, the staggered huff breaking the tense silence.

'You're not the only one at fault here, Conall.' She looked at her feet, scared to admit the pathetic truth but knowing she had to. 'I was willing to accept so little from you,' she said, her voice soft but firm. She needed to admit her part in all this. 'Maybe you didn't tell me the truth about Ross. But you told me you couldn't love me, that you didn't even believe in love.'

She raised her head, knowing she had to look him in the eye, for her own salvation as much as his. 'And yet I was willing to marry you—even to have a child with you—without once demanding more. I've always accepted less than I needed—from my mother, my father, my brother, even Tom—and I did the same with you. And that's on me.'

He'd probably brought her here to try and persuade her that his offer of marriage, the suggestion they have children together, hadn't just been about her connection to Ross. She'd given it some thought over the last two weeks—well, a heck of a lot of thought, to be honest—and she had come to realise he hadn't been lying about that. Her reaction after she had discovered the truth had been about her own insecurities as much as his lack of openness about Ross's connection to his sister. After all, he'd outlined in forensic detail exactly why he had wanted to marry her, to have children with her, all those weeks ago when they'd first slept together. She was the one who had taken that practical explanation and tried to make it mean more.

She brushed away the errant tear that leaked from her eye, knowing despite the pain she was a stronger woman than she had ever been before.

'But I can't… I won't…' She paused, took a breath. 'If you've brought me here to tell me your offer of marriage…' she swallowed heavily '… of a family wasn't just about getting your revenge on Ross, I've already figured that out for myself. But I'm afraid it's not enough to make me change my mind about us. Because I won't settle for less any more.'

Conall shoved his hands in his pockets, the sick feeling of dread in his stomach, tempered by the painful burst of longing, making his ribs hurt as his heart thundered in his chest.

Had she ever looked more magnificent than she did in this moment? The exhaustion in her eyes did nothing to dim the aura of strength and beauty that emanated from her like a bright, shining light.

He'd always known she was smart, funny, captivating and hot enough to make him ache constantly… But had he ever really realised what an amazing woman she was? Not just intelligent, compassionate and kind, but also so strong?

She was telling him where he could shove his proposal of marriage at the exact same moment he had figured out how much he needed her bright, shining light in his life. It would be ironic…if it weren't so terrifying.

He fisted his fingers, resisting the urge to touch her dewy skin, to kiss the sprinkle of freckles across her nose that had always fascinated him, to take her to those places she'd only ever gone with him, to use their electric chemistry to stop her from looking too closely…at him. At them.

But he knew he didn't have the right to touch her again until he made amends for all the wrongs he'd done her, which he knew now were legion… Because he'd had two never-ending weeks to tally up every single one in a mental ledger entitled, *How Conall O'Riordan Screwed Up the Best Thing that Ever Happened to Him.*

He'd planned to start off by telling her his offer of marriage hadn't been about Ross, or Carmel, or Mac. That he'd all but forgotten about his anger with her brother when the guy had appeared out of the blue in the bar at the

Opera House. But she'd already nixed that easy out. And anyway, he knew it was a whole lot more complicated than the lies and omissions, the things he hadn't told her and the things he should have.

'Understood,' he said, because he could see she was waiting for an answer.

'Okay, then,' she said. But when her shoulders drooped and she went to walk past him again, he said the only thing he could think of that would stop her—the God's honest truth.

'Truly, Katherine, I think I fell in love with you the very first day I met you.'

'You…what?' She stopped, her eyes widening as she stared at him. The doubt on her face hurt as it occurred to him that, while she was all the things he couldn't live without, she had no idea of her own worth. And that was on him too. And every other person in her life who hadn't given her what she deserved.

That ends now.

And, just like that, the one thing he'd dreaded having to say, the feelings he'd avoided even acknowledging to himself, let alone her, came pouring out without any filter at all.

'I didn't realise it at the time, because…' He hitched his shoulders, the complete shock on her face making it somehow easier to admit how badly he'd screwed up.

'I was a man who had always convinced myself love wasn't needed. That it was a trap, a burden best avoided. My father tried to make me understand, but I wouldn't listen. He told me over and over again women were the best of us, that they had to be honoured and respected and cherished and protected, and I took that literally. But he wasn't talking about women as such, what he was really talking about was love.'

'He sounds like an incredible man,' she said gently and touched his arm, the soft brush of her fingertips like a balm. 'I know how hard it was on you to lose him.'

He could see the unguarded compassion which was so much a part of her personality. It would be so easy right now to tell her about his mother, about how he'd been the one to find her that awful Christmas morning. To unburden himself of all the guilt, fear and trauma that still haunted him from that terrible discovery—how badly he'd let his mother down, because he'd blamed her for something she'd never had any control over. And maybe he would tell Katherine one day, because he knew she'd listen, and know exactly the right things to say to finally help that young lad put the pain, sadness and guilt to rest.

But he bit down on his lip and kept that darkness inside for now, because he knew if he told her about that terrible day now a part of him would still be using her compassion against her, manipulating her emotions to avoid having to bare his soul completely, and he couldn't do that any more. Not when he loved her so much.

So he satisfied himself with tugging one hand out of his pocket and gathering her fingertips in his. He lifted her hand to press his lips to her knuckles. He felt the inevitable shudder of response and found the strength to smile.

But for once, instead of exploiting their devastating chemistry, he dropped her hand from his mouth and told her what he should have told her weeks ago.

'He *was* an incredible man, and an incredible da,' he said. 'Because he was brave and honest and unafraid of love. Just like you are.'

'What are you trying to say?' she asked, but he could see the hope shining in her eyes again, and he knew he'd already been forgiven.

As the joy surged through him, he promised himself he would never, ever take this feeling for granted again. He would never belittle it, or ignore it, or side-line it, or try to argue himself out of it. Or be afraid of it. Never. Because protecting himself wasn't as important as protecting her.

'Ah, *mo mhuirnín*,' he murmured, lifting his other hand out of his pocket to cradle her cheek, letting all the love he felt show in his eyes. 'Isn't it obvious? I'm trying to tell you I absolutely adore you. And I know I always will.'

She still looked taken aback, but he could see she believed him now because, as well as being smart, beautiful and strong, his one true love was also remarkably intuitive.

What a woman!

'Really?' she said, the way she had the first day he'd met her, but the doubt had disappeared.

'Yes, really,' he said without pause or equivocation. '*Now* will you please marry me?'

The smile that spread across her face was like a beam of sunshine on a rainy day, bringing with it rainbows and pots of gold—*but no leprechauns, thank god.* 'I suppose so,' she said as if she were playing hard to get, but the joy sparking in her eyes told him everything he needed to know.

'Thank goodness.' He banded his arms around her waist and lifted her off the floor.

His whoop of joy joined her gasp of delight as he swung her around then deposited her back on her feet.

Their mouths met, sure and eager. The kiss turned from sweet to carnal in a heartbeat but he made himself make one final vow—before his mind turned to more urgent stuff.

I vow to show her how much I value her, cherish her and love her, every single day for the rest of our lives. Do you hear me, Da?

* * * * *

Caught-up in the magic of
The Billionaire's Proposition in Paris?
Look out for the next instalment in the
Secrets of Billionaire Siblings duet.
In the meantime, check out these other
Heidi Rice stories!

My Shocking Monte Carlo Confession
A Forbidden Night with the Housekeeper
The Royal Pregnancy Test
Innocent's Desert Wedding Contract
One Wild Night with Her Enemy

Available now!